LOVE RULE #1

...s of finding love at
...ty are slim to none.

...and slim went home.

Emma Jackson
RR 1
Hamilton, Missouri

LOVE RULE #5

Love is listening.
Really listening.

#6

...e
...'t
...ad.

Emma Jackson
RR 1
HAmilton, Missouri
64644

...E

..., or

So, if you want someone to like you,
stay on the other side of the fence.

Emma Jackson
RR 1
Hamilton, Missouri
64 6...

love Rule #7

...e is not a feeling

LOVE RULE

...one should make
...ourself more when
...hem.

Emma Jackson
RR 1
Hamilton, Missouri
64644

love Rule #3

The one you don't want to call you
...l call, and the one you're
... call you won't.

...e secret to love is
...ing the person you
...e you.

Rule #4

The trouble with love in the real world is that there's no background music.

Emma Jackson
RR 1
Hamilton, Missouri
64644

Emma Jackson
RR 1
Hamilton, Missouri
64644

CALIFORNIA

TYNDALE HOUSE
PUBLISHERS
WHEATON, ILLINOIS
thirsty(?)

Love Rules

BY
DANDI DALEY MACKALL

To:
Emma Jackson
RR 1
Hamilton, Missouri
64644

Love Rule #2

Love controls your mind and makes you think constantly about the one you love.

Auntie Em
Hamilton, Missouri 64644

Edited by Ramona Cramer Tucker

Designed by Jackie Noe

thirsty(?) is a trademark of Tyndale House Publishers, Inc.

Scripture quotations are taken from the *Holy Bible*, New Living Translation, copyright © 1996. Used by permission of Tyndale House Publishers, Inc., Wheaton, Illinois 60189. All rights reserved.

Library of Congress Cataloging-in-Publication Data

Mackall, Dandi Daley.
  Love rules / Dandi Daley Mackall.
    p. cm.
    Summary: Two college freshmen attempt to write home about their experiences and finally discover the thing that their friend and sister has known all along.
    ISBN 0-8423-8727=7
[1. Dating (Social customs)—Fiction. 2. Brothers and sisters—Fiction. 3. College students—Fiction. 4. Friendship—Fiction.] I. Title.
  PZ7.M1905Lo2005
  [Fic]—dc22   2004015566

Printed in the United States of America

09 08 07 06 05
7   6   5   4   3   2   1

Thanks for your encouragement
on this one.

How I love to make you laugh!

To my daughter, Jen

Thanks to Karen Watson at Tyndale, for giving me a free rein to write a stand alone on this important topic.

Thanks to Ramona Cramer Tucker, for such professional and careful editing.

And thanks to Tyndale House for getting behind this book.

Tyndale House

Mattie

There are some moments that are perfect. I'm only 17, and I know this. Sitting on the hood of the old Ford, wedged between Emma and her brother, Jake, I lean back against the windshield. I can't even guess how many times the three of us have come to this exact spot. First, on our bikes…and later, when Jake got his license, in his car. I want to memorize every detail—the stars, white explosions on blue-black sky, their blurred reflections on the reservoir lake, rippled by the late summer breeze.

I inhale sugar clover, lake grass, and pine, scents as familiar to me as Mom's Jack Daniels or Emma's lavender perfume. I fight the growing weight, the realization that this is the last night the three of us will be together like this. Emma and Jake Jackson and me, Mattie Mays—The Three Musketeers, The Three Stooges, Three Coins in a Fountain.

"Crickets, Emma," I say, making sure she can see my lips. I raise my arm and sign it, just in case. "A train whistle far away. A plop from a fish flopping in the reservoir."

Emma nods, as if she knows exactly what everything sounds

like. For the millionth time, I wonder how my friend, deaf from birth, takes in the sounds I've always tried to describe for her.

Jake sits up straighter. His legs are so long, they hang over the hood. Emma and I quit growing before high school. Jake's still at it. Big, athletic, with thick, sandy blond hair, he has never looked much like his sister. Emma, with thin, fine, red hair, has always been small and frail—even before she was diagnosed with lupus. When Jake was 12, he could hold us both at the same time, one under each arm, tucked away like footballs.

"Frogs," Jake says. "Hear them?" He leans around me to sign for Emma while he talks. "Seriously adolescent frogs. Croaks are coming from down the hill and across the reservoir."

Emma's hands move in the moonlight as she finger spells *cacophony*. She has the tiniest fingers I've ever seen. Her size-four class ring, the smallest the ring company had to offer, has to be worn on her index finger, with tape wound on the underside. She's been in remission for two years.

Perfect, Em signs. *It's a perfect going-away night for you guys.*

"It still makes me mad that we didn't get to graduate together," I complain. The school made me skip my sophomore year in high school, which put me in Jake's class instead of Emma's. Hamilton, Missouri, population 1,701 before the shoe factory closed, had never had a student score "near perfect" on national exams. The teachers tried to make me skip two years and go straight to the senior class, but I drew the line.

Still, instead of experiencing graduation with Emma, I had to walk across the Penney High stage and receive my diploma with Jake and his buddies, and a bunch of girls—like Valerie Ramsey—who acted like I'd shoved and bullied my way into their perfect-without-me class. Crossing the stage with them, I felt like a platypus in a heron parade. Em and her parents clapped as loud for me as they did for Jake, though.

Mom was a no-show.

It was the Jacksons who went to all the trouble of having a going-away party for Jake *and* me tonight. We hung around until our friends—mostly Jake's friends—left. Then Emma called for a moon check, and we sneaked away to the reservoir, just outside town. Sometimes I think moon checks have saved my life. I know. Pretty dramatic. But I've had my share of pretty dramatic nights, when I couldn't stand it in the house with Mom or with her "friends." I'd call Jake, and all I'd say was "I need a moon check." And he and Emma would be outside waiting for me by the time I got my jacket on.

Only thing that would have made this night more perfect, Emma signs, *would have been my big brother coming through with Paul McCartney tickets.*

"Don't blame me!" Jake protests. "Blame Dennis." Jake turns to me. "Did he tell you he got the last ticket—a front-row seat, no less?"

Dennis did tell me. If he'd been able to get two tickets, he was going to take me with him. We'd dated some our senior year.

"You can't blame Dennis," I tell Jake, "just because he succeeded where you failed."

"Hey, I did everything except ask the girl at the ticket counter to marry me," Jake says, signing at the same time.

"To marry you? Why didn't you just offer her good old cash?" I tease.

"I did!" Jake whines. "I would have sold my computer—or your hair—to get us tickets to McCartney."

Jake has ragged me about my hair since I was too little to brush it myself. My hair has always been abnormally thick and wild, "like a deranged Scottish woman, wandering the hills for her lost love." So says Jake. Everybody else claims they'd kill for naturally curly, coal black hair like mine. I don't much care one way or the other. But if Jake's right, and I *have* been looking for my lost love, I haven't found him.

"Should have sold your own golden locks, Jake Jackson," I counter. "Might as well. How old was your dad when *he* lost *his* hair?"

"That's hitting low, even for you, Matt," Jake complains. "But if you want to talk hair—"

Stop, you two! Emma's fingers shout, snapping from her palm as if they're on springs.

3

We're quiet for a few minutes. The steady cricket chirping overtakes us in waves, as if someone's playing with the volume control on the cricket sound track. I can't help wondering when I'll hear crickets like this again.

In the morning Jake and I will leave Hamilton and drive cross-country to Los Angeles to start classes at Freedom University. I would do just about anything to smuggle Emma into my suitcase.

I grab Em's hand and slide off the hood, taking her with me. Together we run down the hill, shedding our shoes before we reach the water.

"Come on, Jake!" I slide, as the ground turns mushy under my toes.

"You're crazy!" Jake hollers back.

Emma rolls up her jeans, and I do the same. The Big and Little Dippers wink down at us. In one glance I take in Cassiopeia's M and Orion's armor.

We step through cattails into silk-bottomed water, so cold the shock tingles my feet and travels to my fingertips.

Emma frowns and jerks her head toward Jake.

I pass the command. "Jake, you better get down here right now!"

Grumbling, Jake thunders down the hill and kicks off his shoes. Then he trudges into the water and stops between us.

We stand there in ankle-deep water that barely moves. I can almost feel Emma praying. Everything I know about God, I've gotten from her. The world feels as if Emma's God is holding his breath, waiting for something. Jake's waiting too. I can tell he's watching his sister's hand, as if expecting a divine message.

Slowly Em stretches out her arm so we can both read her fingers by moonlight. *I want you to promise me something.*

"Name it, Em." I struggle to hold myself together.

This year, while I'm finishing high school, you two have to be my ears and my eyes. Experience life for me! I need that to be a great writer.

I can't speak. Em has wanted to be a writer since before she could hold a pencil. She has so much talent. *She* should be the one going off to college.

"We'll e-mail you every day, Em," Jake promises, signing it as he speaks.

That's great. But I want more.

I can sense that she's going somewhere with this. I've always been able to tell when Em has something worked out and is just waiting for the rest of us to catch up—like the time she roped Jake and me into putting on a jitterbug exhibition in the community theater. By the time she let us in on her plan, the event was on the front page of the *Hamiltonian*. Emma definitely has an agenda now.

"Out with it," I beg. "You know we'll do anything."

Love, she answers. It's a simple hand sign, the first Emma taught me—arms crossed over her heart. *I want to know everything you learn about love.*

"Be careful what you wish for," Jake jokes.

Emma laughs, then signs, *Trust me. I have no interest in the details of your love life, big brother. I want research, but not that kind.*

"I don't get it, Em," I say.

I want you to go off to the university and discover the truth about love. Observe it. Live it. Figure it out.

"Oh, is that all?" Jake splashes her, then hurries toward safe ground.

Em's fingers snap together, and Jake turns back. *No! I want you two to get together once a week and come up with a principle you've discovered about love. A rule a week.*

This is so Em. "You want us to e-mail you love rules?" I ask.

No! Her fingers and thumb snap together again, signing no. *E-mail is great, better than the phone for me, right? But as a writer, I don't consider e-mail messages as writing. People use a small i and misspell things intentionally. It's like chatter. I want something permanent, something I can save in my writing files and journals. I want . . .* Her eyes grow big, as if she's only now thought of this brilliant idea. *Postcards! Get together once a week and send me a postcard.*

"But what if we don't see each other during the week?" I ask. "L.A. isn't Hamilton, you know. Jake and I aren't just going to bump into each other."

Emma has her answer ready. *Okay. Then promise me you'll get together every Monday night, no matter what. Send me one "Love Rule" every week you're away.*

Jake and I exchange skeptical looks.

You asked what you could do for me, Emma signs. She gives us her pitiful puppy look. *This is it. This is all I'm asking.*

She looks at Jake and finally gets a nod. Then she turns to me.

I've never been able to say no to Emma Jackson. I sigh. "Deal."

Good! she signs. Then her hands clap above her head before her fingers spell *LOVE RULES!*

2

We Three Stooges wade to shore and race up the hill, picking up shoes on the way and throwing them at each other. When we get to the car, Emma's fingers move again, and her thin body starts to weave in rhythm to a tune only she can hear. She signs, *"He's a real nowhere man—living in his nowhere land—making all his nowhere plans for nobody."* Her hands flow, finger dancing in the moonlight.

I jump in, signing and singing, louder than the frogs and crickets put together. Then Jake joins us for the chorus. We sing Beatles songs to the hills of Hamilton, to the reservoir, where we've been swimming and skating more times than there are fish in the water.

None of Emma's other friends get it. They can't understand how Emma, who has never heard the Beatles sing, could love them so much. But Jake and I have watched Em tap her foot in perfect beat to loud music. She feels it. We've danced for hours to *Abbey Road* in my garage, Em's favorite place to listen to music because the vibrations ricochet off the concrete and metal.

Emma Jackson owns every video and DVD ever made of the Beatles. She sits cross-legged, inches from the screen, so she can read their lips.

The Beatles have always made my top-five-favorites list, but they have never wavered from Emma's #1 spot. She deserves to see McCartney in concert—tonight.

I slap the hood of the car. "Come on! We're going to a concert!" I open the driver's door and hold out my palm. "Keys, Jake."

Jake doesn't budge. "They're sold out, Matt. Dear ol' Dennis got the last ticket. Remember?"

"Who needs tickets? Keys, Jake! I mean it. Hurry up, you two!"

Emma moves to the passenger side. *The concert will be over by the time we get there*, she signs.

Jake groans, but he tosses me his keys. "Something tells me we're taking a little drive."

"In!" I climb behind the wheel and turn the key. I've been driving Jake's car since before I had my license.

Emma buckles in front, and Jake takes the back.

"Emma's right, Matt," Jake complains. "The concert will be over before we get there."

I shift to reverse and adjust the mirrors. "No way. Paul McCartney gives his audience their money's worth. He'll do a dozen curtain calls." I back out to the gravel lane that leads out of the reservoir park. "Jake, put on your seat belt."

It drives me crazy that an 18-year-old isn't smart enough to fasten his seat belt. But *smart* isn't really the problem. I'm not sure when I figured out that Jake Jackson liked taking risks—most of them a lot more serious than seat belts. Jake has always been the first to take a dare, no matter how stupid it is. He was the first to see if a growling dog meant business, and the last to come in out of an electrical storm.

Jake frowns at me in the rearview mirror, but I hear his seat belt snap.

"Call your parents and tell them we'll be really late," I order. Jake and Emma have great parents. Mr. and Mrs. Jackson freak out if they don't know where their kids are. I seriously wonder how they'll handle it when Jake's too far away to keep track of. I wonder how Jake will handle it.

I cut across to old 36 and catch I-35 near Cameron. Then it's smooth sailing all the way to Kansas City, about 40 miles. We sing Beatles songs the whole drive. Emma knows every lyric to every song. She mouths the words and signs, her hands swaying above her head.

Once we hit the city, I exit for the American Royal building. When Em and I were little, we dreamed of having our own horses. We were so horse crazy that we nagged Em's parents until they took us to the big American Royal Horse Show. They still have the horse show there, but other events use the giant center too.

"So what's the plan?" Jake hollers up from the backseat.

I hear the excitement in his voice. He's probably psyched, thinking we're going to break in.

"Follow my lead," I instruct, whizzing past full parking lots. "And look important."

They're still playing! Emma signs. *Nobody's leaving the parking lot.*

I drive past all the packed parking lots. It's so late that I don't think people suspect us of barging in. I ease to the side of the building and stop about 100 feet from the side entrance. Then I shut off the engine and toss Jake the keys. "Wait for my signal," I command, getting out of the car. "Then look famous." I start to go, then jog back to the car. "I need your cell, Jake."

A line winds around the building from as far as I can see, right up to the side entrance, which looks more like a fire-escape exit. When Counting Crows came here for a concert, Em and I stood in this very line, the "hangers-on" line, comprised of people who can't get tickets but come anyway, hoping. When we couldn't get in, we left and went back home. But these hangers-on aren't leaving. They've stayed in hopes of catching a glimpse of the famous Beatle, or maybe hearing bits of the concert through the door, if it ever opens.

I pull up the collar on my white shirt and reach back to twist my hair on top of my head. Then I stroll closer to the side entrance so I can get a better look at the six-foot, 260-pound mountain man, who has to be the bouncer. Before he can see me, I skirt around the building to the next entrance.

The next side door is equally guarded, with a slightly shorter line of hopefuls. Ignoring the glares from the waiting line, I sidle up to the middle-aged security guard, who's dressed in a black turtleneck, black pants, and a black Kangol hat. He's standing in front of the door, four steps above me.

I smile up at him until he looks down. When he does, I grin sheepishly.

The guard gives me a goofy grin. He's missing a tooth, though I pretend not to notice. He stands a little straighter and nods at me.

Guys are beyond strange. I've never had a real boyfriend, but I've dated enough to observe the species. They are their own worst enemies.

"That is *such* a great hat!" I exclaim to the guard and then glance away, as if too shy to look at him directly.

He tips his hat. "Yeah? It works for me."

"Are you part of the show?" I'm wide-eyed with admiration.

He shrugs. "Nah. Not really."

"What's your name?" I ask.

"Stan. What's yours?"

"Thanks, Stan." I smile and trot off to the next entrance.

With a similar routine, and almost zero effort, I glean the names of two other security guards. Then I race back to the first door, stopping long enough to wave at Emma and Jake, who are still in the car.

Finally I march purposefully to the side entrance guarded by the husky bouncer, who may very well be gainfully employed by our own Kansas City mafia. "Excuse me," I say, slipping in front of the first hopeful in line. I duck under the rope and trot up the four steps to the bouncer. Close up, I have to change my estimate of his weight to 300 pounds.

He lumbers toward me. "Hey!"

"Hey," I return, but much friendlier. I glance at my watch. "Sorry, Love. I know. You're overdue for your break. Not my fault.

Stan took advantage. I thought the bloke was never coming back."
My British accent has popped up, all on its own. It does that sometimes, although I've never set foot in England. On occasion the
same thing happens with my French, German, and Polish accents.
I guess I pick them up from movies, and they stick with me, tucked
away in my accent closet until I put them on, like costumes, whenever the mood strikes.

The first hanger-on in line tries to follow my lead and sneak
under the rope.

"Here now!" I scold. "What are you on about? None of that."

Reluctantly she returns to her place in line.

The bouncer frowns down at me. "Who are you?"

"Liz." I reach over and take his hand, shaking it, without his
consent. "Break relief?"

"I didn't know anything about break relief."

"No? Lovely." I shrug. "Leroy took too long anyway. I've
worked my hours. And John didn't even take a smoke. He hit on
me the whole 20 minutes. I don't have to take that." I nod to the
group of middle-aged women at the front of the hopeful line and get
their approving, supportive nods back.

"So if you don't want a break, I'll push off." I start down the
steps and am about to duck under the rope when he calls me back.

"Wait a minute! *I* want a break. I need a drink."

Yes! I turn and trudge back to the door. "Right." I check my
wrist, hoping he can't see that there's no watch there. "Twenty
minutes, yeah? Don't be a Leroy. I stood there an hour."

"Okay. Deal." The guard opens the door and disappears
inside. When McCartney notes escape and waft out to the grateful
hangers-on, the line cheers. We get at least four bars of "Help!"
before the door slams shut.

I take my position in front of the door and imitate the security
goon—legs apart, one hand behind my back. After a minute I dive
for the cell in my waistband, as if it's ringing. "Right," I say into the
dead phone. "What vehicle?" I gaze around until I see Jake's car.
"It's here." Pause. "Got it. Over."

I wave at the car, motioning for Jake and Emma to come on over. "VIPs," I confide to the hopefuls.

"Who are they?" asks a woman who might be the same age as my mom, although this woman looks at least 10 years younger.

"I'm not allowed to say," I answer as Emma and Jake strut toward us, arm in arm.

"Sorry, Love!" I shout when they head for the front doors. "I'm afraid you'll have to use this entrance."

Jake appears to be asking the charming, slight waif on his arm if this would be acceptable. The waif flicks her wrist in displeasure but lets herself be led past the line of hopefuls to the roped-off steps.

I hurry down the steps to unhook the rope and let Emma and Jake walk through before I re-snap it. Then I trot up to get the door for the VIPs. "Wait for me," I whisper to Jake as they breeze past.

"Enjoy!" I exclaim.

"Thank you, dearie," Jake says, making a show of slipping me a fiver.

I pocket the cash. "Thank *you*!"

Again the brief exodus of the band's music brings applause from the hopefuls.

"Please tell me who he is!" begs a woman too old for the ponytail she's sporting. She was third in line but now crowds ahead of #2.

I peer around, like someone might be spying. Then I lean toward the hopefuls. "Jake Jackson."

The woman first in line looks puzzled. "I don't know him. Is he a movie star? He's cute enough."

I can't help grinning. I've never thought of Jake as movie-star cute, but I have to admit that most of the Penney High females probably have had crushes on him at one time or another.

"Oh, *I* know who he is!" declares Aging Ponytail. "Jake Jackson is so neat! Isn't he that actor, in that movie . . . what's it called? With that long-haired actress . . . what's her name?"

"Say now! You didn't hear that from me." I wink at Ponytail. "I have a favor to ask you, Love. What's your name now?"

"Marianne," Ponytail answers, inching her way first in line.

"I hate to ask you. I keep giving all the security lads breaks, but nobody gives *me* one. I need to go to the loo. Will you cover the door for me?"

"Me?"

"Yeah. If Paul comes out this way, somebody needs—"

"Paul? He might come out here? Do you think so?" Marianne has already shoved her way ahead of First-in-Line. Now she fumbles with the rope guarding the steps.

"Too right. If he gets here before the other security guard gets back, you could ask Paul to wait."

"Me? Ask Paul to wait?" She unfastens the rope and hops up the steps. "You go on. Leave it to me."

"Brilliant." With a grateful nod I duck inside.

Emma and Jake are waiting inside the door.

"Thought you'd never get here," Jake says, grinning.

I ram him with my shoulder. "Yeah? Well, if you think you're getting your tip money back, Love, think again."

Em is signing something, but I can't see. My eyes aren't used to the dim light yet.

It only takes one more impersonation to get us close to the stage. I grab a handful of programs and usher Emma and Jake front row, center. Nobody stays seated on the floor of a McCartney concert, so we fit right in, easing into the mass of bodies, screaming and dancing in the aisles.

"Matt!" Jake points to the end of the row, where Dennis is waving at us. He looks out of place here, and I have a feeling the only reason he's at the concert is because his dad told him it was a waste of hard-earned money.

I wave back at Dennis and wonder how many years on the farm it will take him to turn into his father—not that that would be a horrible thing. Dennis is never happier than when he's down on the farm.

McCartney finishes the last refrain of "Yesterday" and breaks into "All You Need is Love."

Before I can clue Emma which song is starting, she's already *singing* along with Paul. Her green eyes sparkle. Her tiny arms wave above her head and her fingers dance in strobe light.

I keep one eye on the great McCartney and one eye on my friend. Em doesn't miss a word or a beat. Then her fingers break with the rhythm and spell, *Thank you, God. Now it really is perfect*.

I feel someone bump into me—Dennis.

A grin flicks at his lips. He's pretty cute. "Hey, Mattie. Jake offered me a ride home. Looks like we'll get our McCartney date after all."

Dennis the Date

It's nice riding in the backseat with Mattie. She's not like other girls I've gone out with. Mattie never makes me feel like a dumb farm boy. She's easy to talk to. I wish she'd stay in Hamilton, like me. She doesn't have to run off to California and college and everything.

Jake swerves between the long lines of concert traffic trying to leave the parking lots. His sister, Emma, signs something at him. And he answers her, "Take it easy, Emma."

"Guess we should have left before the last song," I comment, thinking about how mad my dad's going to be when I get home and how tired I'm going to be when he wakes me up at dawn to bale hay.

"No complaints, Dennis," Mattie warns. "We'll toss you back onto that Greyhound bus. You should have known your dad wouldn't let you take the truck for a McCartney concert."

Dad and I hadn't fought. Not with words anyway. He just said the whole thing was dumb and that I couldn't use the truck. I said fine and took the bus.

"Worked out," I say now, putting my arm around Mattie. "We get one last date, right?"

She grins, and I figure Mattie Mays was the prettiest girl in high school, even though she wasn't any more popular than I was. It was almost like she was too much for Penney High —too pretty, too smart, too ambitious. She didn't fit here. I do. Still, she could have stayed here and had an okay life. Her mother's the town drunk, but Mattie could have moved out of her mother's place. I could do a lot worse than marry the likes of Mattie Mays.

"Have you thought any more about taking ag classes at Warrensburg?" Mattie asks.

Emma turns and smiles. She signs something, and Mattie interprets. "Emma says Central Missouri State has a great agricultural program."

"I'm going to work the farm for a while," I answer. I wasn't that good in high school, and I can't see going to college to learn about farming, when I've been doing it all my life. "Don't see why you guys have to go to California for school. Plenty of good schools in Missouri."

Not only are Jake and Mattie going to Freedom University, but so is Valerie Ramsey, the superintendent's daughter. She and Jake dated on and off all through high school, but it's weird the three of them would end up at the same school.

"California lured us out there," Mattie says. "I think their governor told them they had to beef up their Midwestern quota."

Emma signs again, and this time Jake interprets. "Freedom University gave Mattie a full scholarship with a work-study job to cover expenses."

"How about you, Jake?" I ask. "Didn't Mizzou recruit you hard for their basketball program?"

"Yeah," Jake admits. "But Emma dared me to apply to Freedom."

Mattie leans forward and signs to Emma, as she asks, "Did you really dare Jake to go to Freedom?"

Emma grins, then signs something back. Mattie laughs, then leans back and whispers to me, "Em says she dared Jake to go to Freedom—*before* she heard Val was going there."

I nod. Mattie and Valerie have never liked each other.

Valerie's the one who started the rumor last year that Mattie's mother was arrested for prostitution. Turned out it was just drunk driving—one night in jail.

"Did Emma admit daring me to Freedom?" Jake asks.

"Yep," Mattie answers, winking at me. "Anyway, I'm glad you're going, Jake. At least I'll know one person there."

"Two," Jake corrects. "Don't forget Valerie."

"Who could forget Valerie?" Mattie asks, signing something to Emma.

Emma makes little mouse noises, trying not to laugh.

Jake finally breaks free of concert traffic, and they start reliving every song they heard McCartney sing. Then Mattie pumps me for details about every song they missed, and the rest of the drive, they sing most of them.

When we pull into sleepy Hamilton, Jake keeps going up deserted Main Street instead of turning off for the farm. Penney High was named after our only famous resident, J.C. Penney. Even he moved out when he was young and started his stores in other cities.

I watch the school as Jake inches past. I've never liked school much. But as we roll by and the brick building gets smaller and smaller in the rear window, I can't help thinking I may have left the best days of my life there.

Mattie is turned in the seat, staring out the back window, even though we can't see the school any longer. I can't read her face—if she's sad to leave or happy to be rid of the place. I never could read her. I wonder if anybody can.

Jake circles back and takes the dirt road to the farm.

"Thanks for the ride, Jake. Emma, I'll see you around." I think she can read my lips, but I make a point to nod directly at her. Then I smile at Mattie. "Walk me to the door, Mattie?"

"You got it." She climbs out of the backseat after me.

We cross the yard and my old collie runs up, barking. "Easy, Lassie!" I call to her.

"Lassie? Think of that name all by yourself, did you?" Mattie teases.

We walk up the porch steps, and I see Dad's shadow pull back from the window. I knew he'd wait up.

Mattie glances back at Jake's car. "Well, Dennis, you be careful. Let's keep in touch, okay?"

I grin at her, but I think we both know we won't keep in touch. I feel like I've missed something with Mattie. I lean down and kiss her. "Tell Jake to drive careful. We'll see you, Mattie."

I walk inside and wonder if Mattie Mays will ever be back.

Mattie

Soon as I'm back in the car Emma signs, *So, did Dennis declare his undying love for you?*

"Of course," I answer, grinning. Emma knows that Dennis and I were only convenience dates, somebody to go to the prom and homecoming with. I don't think the guy ever gave me a second thought, except when he needed somebody to go to a dance with him. He's not a bad dancer . . . for a farmer.

"Of course, what?" Jake asks, turning the car around.

Before I can come up with an answer, Emma signs, *Sorry, big brother. You wouldn't understand.*

We're unusually silent when Jake pulls into his driveway. I try to memorize the Jackson house, which has felt more like home to me than Mom's apartment. I love my mother, and I'm sure she loves me, as much as she can love anybody. But when I get homesick, this is the home I'll be *sick* for.

I have slept over at Emma's a hundred times. Emma has slept at my house exactly once, and that was a disaster neither of us spoke of afterward. It was when we were in sixth grade, and Mom was dating John the Demolition Derby man. He and Mom got into it that night, and Em and I ended up calling Mrs. Jackson to come get us.

The Jacksons are asleep when we creep in the back way. Jake says good night, and Em and I get ready for bed, then stretch out on her king-sized bed. Moonlight streams through the bay window. Emma's room is as familiar to me as my own. It smells of cinnamon and lavender and makes me think of the saying about "sugar and spice and everything nice."

Em lifts her arm, and I watch her fingers by the light of the moon. *Can't sleep again?*

I sign back, finger spelling, *Somniphobia*.

Fear of falling asleep, Em signs. She shakes her head. Emma has been around me long enough to recognize most of the phobias I toss out to the general public, and all of them I assign to us. At one time or another, I've accused Em of *motorphobia*, a fear of automobiles—she thinks Jake and I drive too fast. Also, *papyrophobia*, fear of paper—an affliction that seemed to strike when we had long term papers due. And *porphyrophobia*, fear of purple—when we switched out of our we-love-pink-and-purple phase and moved directly into the we-hate-pink-and-purple stage. We've analyzed Jake as a *peladophobe*, one who fears bald people. And a *bibliophobe*, someone who fears books—because Em and I read all the time. And even an *allodoxaphobe*, one who fears strong opinions.

Somniphobia is the only fear I admit to. "Maybe if they didn't call it *falling* asleep, I'd have half a chance of getting a good night of it," I suggest.

So who needs sleep anyway? Emma signs. *When I wake up in the middle of the night, I figure God has something to say to me. So I listen. I love the middle of the night.*

I envy Emma her talks with God. I get more from the overflow of her relationship with God than I do from my own. How could I not believe in her Jesus? But in all the sleepless nights I've had, it never once occurred to me to pray.

Mattie, Em signs, rolling over onto her back, her arm stretched high, *what do you want out of college?*

If anyone else asked that question, I'd whip off a witty answer, brimming with sarcasm. Em says my sharp tongue is the reason I didn't have many friends, or dates, in high school. But Emma deserves an honest answer. I know exactly what I want out of college, even though I've hardly admitted it to myself. "Love."

Emma's eyes narrow to slits of emeralds. Then her fingers move. *Are you saying that because I'm making you come up with Love Rules?*

I shake my head slowly. I've been thinking about love more and more since graduation. If I were talking to anyone else, I wouldn't let a thought out unless I'd sharpened it first. But I allow myself to think aloud with Em. "I want the usual things too. I need great grades to keep my scholarship. And I want a career out of the deal. I'll become a lawyer. Or a doctor. Or a teacher. Or someone who works on Wall Street. It doesn't really matter, does it?"

Em laughs. It's the only time she lets the world hear the little bit of voice she has. The sound is nasal, broken. And I will miss it more than anything else when I'm in L.A. without her.

"You know what I mean, Em. I'm not worried about that part." If Valerie Ramsey heard me say that, she'd call me egotistical and arrogant. Among other reasons, Valerie hates me because she would have ended up valedictorian if I hadn't skipped a grade and "robbed her of the honor." Big, fat honor to be #1 out of 58 students.

But Em gets me, like nobody else ever has. She knows that, for my whole life, I've been able to *do* things, to perform well, to learn how to be good at almost anything. It's nothing to brag about. It's almost as if it doesn't have anything to do with me or who I am. It's just the way things are. I've been head cook at Curtis Café, a part-time teller at the Hamilton Bank, an off-the-books mechanic at Shaney's Auto Repair, a vet assistant at Doc Snyder's office. I even played basketball on the boys' team in seventh grade. Chemistry and physics come as easily to me as English and creative writing. Job skills aren't the problem.

Em uses her eyes, instead of her hands, to urge me to keep going.

"I want to date a lot. I want a boyfriend, one who's crazy about me." I laugh uneasily.

Em is grinning, but her gaze hasn't eased off. She's waiting for more.

"I want to get love out of college, Em. I want a guy who loves me." I grab a pillow and cover my face with it. I cannot believe I'm saying this stuff. It sounds more like something Val would say.

Emma pulls off the pillow and smiles down at me. I think her eyes are moist. Then she signs, *I get it, Mattie.*

"Do you, Em?" I ask, because I'm not sure I do. I don't think I know what love is, what it feels like to be loved by someone.

You deserve love—a lot more than you've gotten so far, Mattie, Emma signs. *And you're thinking it's about time for you to fall in love.*

"Ugh! There's that word again—*fall*! So I guess I'm not just a *somniphobe*. I'm a *philophobe* too."

Emma shakes her head and signs, *You're not afraid of love. You're just afraid of needing someone besides Mattie Mays.*

Sometimes I think Em knows me better than I know me. She knows I love my mother. She also knows I've had to protect myself from needing my mom—or anybody—for as long as I can remember.

Emma hugs me, then lets go so she can sign. *So that's what I'll pray you get out of college—love—that Mattie Mays finds love at Freedom University!* She yawns once and snuggles under the covers. She's fading, but she sticks up her hand and signs, *Just promise me you'll keep an eye on my brother. And if at all possible, keep Valerie away from him.*

I laugh. Emma Jackson never says anything mean about anybody. But even Em can't help herself when it comes to Val.

I lie on my back, hands clasped behind my neck, and try to imagine what college will be like. In the dark I hear Em's steady breathing.

Maybe it's being in Emma's room—and God really must feel at home here—but for the first time in the middle of the night, I talk to God.

Okay, God. I'm not good at this, not like Emma. But I want you to know I'm taking Em's assignment seriously. I want to discover the Love Rules. So will you help me figure out love while I'm at the university? And could you toss in a great boyfriend while you're at it? You could do that, right? Seriously, how hard can it be?

5

Emma's gone when I wake up. Rhett Butler, the Jacksons' shaggy Irish setter, is lying next to me, whimpering and licking my face. He has serious morning breath.

"I love you too, Rhett." Saying "love" brings back last night's conversation, and I'm kind of embarrassed about it. It helps knowing Emma is the best secret-keeper in the universe.

It's still dark outside, and the room carries the night chill. I haul myself out of bed, wash up, and toss my things into my backpack. Jake told me I could bring everything I wanted and we'd fit it in somehow. But I don't have that much to bring—bedding, clothes, books. The rooms come with computers.

I feel my way down the hall and onto the stairs, but I stop when I hear voices coming from the kitchen. Jake's saying something about me. I tiptoe to the bottom of the stairs, scratching Rhett's ears to keep him from giving me away. It makes me think of another early morning a few years ago when I was sleeping over and woke up before Emma. I heard Mr. and Mrs. Jackson in the kitchen, laughing and chatting about their day ahead. I stopped just like this and spied on them, eavesdropping on normal family life.

Jake's deep voice carries to the stairway. "I'll bet Matt didn't get any sleep, right? So I'm going to have to drive the 1,685 miles by myself?"

I want to move closer so I can see Emma's response. She doesn't let her big brother get away with much.

"I know. I know," Jake says, as if he's defending himself. Em must have let him have it. "I'll be good. Did she call her mother last night?"

The answer is no. We said good-bye yesterday, right before she went out drinking with Brian. If I'd called her last night, she wouldn't have remembered it this morning.

"Good idea," Jake says. I hear the fridge open. "I'll take the apples too. I need better car snacks though. What's in the jelly cupboard? Matt likes those granola bars."

I've eavesdropped long enough. But I still tiptoe across the living room to the kitchen. Light above the sink spreads like a halo, brushing over Emma, who stands looking out the window. From the back my friend looks like a little kid playing dress-up in her mother's pajamas. Jake is staring at her too. My chest tightens.

Emma's arm shoots up, and without turning around, she signs, *Jake, maybe you should wait until it's light. You don't want to hit another deer.*

"I'll be careful." He says it before she turns around. When she does, he says it again. "Besides, we're going to drive straight through. We might as well get started. You want me to go wake Matt up?"

That's my cue. I breeze into the kitchen with Rhett Butler on my heels. I slip off my backpack and drop my duffel bag. "Hey! California, here we come, or what?"

"Something like that," Jake answers.

Emma smiles and signs, *Good morning.* I return the sign, lifting one arm from the other, like a sunrise. It's one of the first signs she taught me.

Rhett, toenails clicking on the linoleum, trots over to Emma for a good morning pat and won't let up until she squats and scruffs him behind the ears.

"Nice shirt," Jake comments.

"This ol' thing?" I grin at him. It's the Freedom sweatshirt he brought me back from his basketball trip out there. "Some jock got it for me."

Jake gazes around the kitchen as if he'll never see it again. "It's so weird. I was only gone two weeks to California for training, but already the Jackson family kitchen looks like something out of my past."

"The Jackson family kitchen looks like something out of everybody's past," I add. This is the room Mrs. Jackson refuses to remodel. Every other room in the house has been redone. But here old-fashioned Formica counters lead to a round wood kitchen table, complete with a rooster napkin holder and chairs Mr. Jackson brought home when his mother "downsized" to the nursing home. Only the appliances are from this decade.

"Let's hit it, Matt," Jake insists.

Mom and Dad? Emma signs furiously.

"I left them a note." He points to a tiny Post-it note on the kitchen table.

"Jake, was that the best you could do?" I scold. His parents deserve a lot more than a two-inch-square good-bye.

"Let them sleep. I'll call them from the road, okay? Cell's all charged. We need to get going."

Emma smiles at Jake, and I get the feeling there's more going on here than Jake in a hurry, like maybe his parents couldn't survive a face-to-face send-off. Em walks over to Jake and reaches up her bony arms. He leans down and hugs her gently, like he's afraid he might break her. Then they back away from each other.

This is the part I've been dreading since I got the acceptance letter. Leaving Emma. I try to keep it light and give her a quick hug, but she doesn't let go. So I give in and hug her back. "I'm going to miss you so much, Em," I whisper, although I know she can't see my lips to hear me.

When she lets go, Emma signs, *Don't forget your promise.*

I better see a postcard in my mailbox every single week. And I expect amazing revelations about love from you two. Love Rules! Now, get out of here. And like it or not, I'll be talking to God about both of you.

As Jake backs the car out , Rhett Butler follows to the end of the drive, then trots back and sits beside Emma. Em stands in the driveway, waving at us with one arm. The other arm is by her side, and I can almost see her fingers moving wildly, gracefully, as she talks to God.

Jake takes the first driving shift while I wrestle with sleep in the passenger seat. The back is filled with Jake's boxes. I try to curl my legs under me and use the window as a pillow. "You know, Jake, I hope your roommate doesn't bring anything, because you're bringing enough for your whole dorm."

"What do you know about it, Matt? I can't believe you didn't bring more stuff. I've dated girls who took more with them to the movies than you're bringing to L.A. for a year. The rooms are pretty big."

I envy Jake, that he's already seen the campus and met his roommate. I've e-mailed mine twice. Her name is Gillian, and she seems nice, but I'm so rotten at making friends. And I've never shared a room with anybody, not that my room in our apartment was anything to brag about. Mom kept her overflow junk in my closet and did wholesale dumping to my room whenever a boyfriend moved in with her.

So Gillian is the one bringing the stereo system, fridge, TV-VCR-DVD, and microwave. She kept asking if I wanted to bring this or that, or if she could. I kept answering that she could go ahead and bring everything. But I hate feeling like I'm already not pulling my weight.

It wears me out not sleeping, so I pretend that I'm asleep, and maybe I do doze in and out. I can't stop thinking about Emma, picturing her in those baggy pajamas that fit her a couple of years ago. Emma was diagnosed with lupus when she was 10 and started being tired all the time. I remember being so scared when her parents were taking her to a specialist that I begged her not to go. I couldn't stand for them to find anything wrong with her. I thought if she was dying, then I wanted to die too.

Since then she's had three flares, with long remissions in between, when nobody would guess that there was anything wrong with her.

"Hello, Kansas," Jake whispers to the Sunflower State. So I figure I must have slept some, if we're through Missouri already.

I feel the sun on my cheek and open my eyes. Outside the window, light pushes through a bank of white-pink clouds. Fields of sunflowers spread from the highway, as far as I can see. "Kansas?"

"Miles and miles and miles of it." Jake yawns. "Did you sleep at all? You didn't exactly snore, but the noises you made were more entertaining than farm reports, which seem to be the only news worth broadcasting on radio stations around here." He looks over at me. "Whoa! Nice hair."

I pull down the visor mirror and try not to laugh. My hair looks like I've stuck my finger in an electrical outlet. "Jake Jackson, you must get over your *caligynephobia*."

Jake raises his eyebrows.

"Fear of beautiful women."

"I'm planning to work hard on that one in California. Look, I'm starving. All I could reach were the apples and plums. The good junk's too far back. I need real food. Like a triple cheeseburger."

I lean over and read Jake's watch. "It's only 9:00."

"Talk to the stomach."

He takes the next exit to the service plaza and pulls up to the gas pump.

"These plazas make me think of cutouts and paper dolls," I complain. "We could be anywhere, and everything would look exactly the same."

"You have a phobia of rest-stop plazas?" Jake gets out of the car. "*Plaza-phobia*? Hand me my wallet out of the glove compartment, Matt."

"I can get this one." I check the price on the pump. It's 10 cents a gallon higher than I'd figured when I calculated how much half of the gas would add up to.

"No." Jake sticks out his hand. "You get the next one. Hurry, Matt. I'm dying of hunger here."

I hand him the wallet and decide that when I'm driving, I'll take us into towns for gas. Prices are bound to be better, and maybe we'll see more of the country than concrete plazas.

I get out of the car and stretch. The pavement feels rough on my bare feet. I shed the sweatshirt and brush a spot of fuzz off my tank top. "I'll take the next shift," I holler to Jake across the Ford.

"Fine with me!" he hollers back. "What do you want to eat?"

"I'm good." I've only got enough to buy one meal a day. Granola bars and fruit will work fine for the rest.

I've been saving for college since I was 14 and had my first steady, non-babysitting job. I washed dishes in the back room at Curtis Café. The first night I came home with wrinkled fingers from too much hot dishwater, I wrote in my diary, "I am getting out of Hamilton. I am going to college." But at least half of what I earned went for groceries or the electric or phone bills. If the scholarship hadn't come through, I'm not sure what I would have done.

Jake comes back and hands me a cup. "There's a biscuit in the bag for you too." He shifts the white sack to his teeth and folds himself into the passenger seat. Setting his coffee in one of the cup holders, he digs into the sack. "I don't want you driving on an empty stomach."

I start the car and take a sip of the cappuccino. "Thanks, Jake."

After three biscuit sandwiches, he's out and snoring. It's hard to believe that one fairly normal human can make so much noise sleeping. I punch on the radio and turn the dial, but there's nothing except country western and static. The static's better.

There's too much time to think when you drive. I try to change the direction of my thoughts, but they keep racing back to my mom. They cut her hours at the glove factory, even though she's worked there for 14 years, since the shoe factory folded. True, she isn't exactly a model employee when she's drinking. But it doesn't seem fair. I don't know how she's going to cover rent and bills and pay the interest on her credit card without me. Brian, her boyfriend, hasn't been paying his share, although Mom says he will. I don't trust him. He's a carbon copy of J.P., her last boyfriend, only without the mustache and cowboy boots. But I don't know what Mom will do if Brian takes off on her. It's hard not to worry about her.

I wonder if this is how most *mothers* feel when they send their kids off to college.

6

When the gas needle hovers over *Empty*, I'm still driving through Kansas. I've passed the time by counting tractors (53) and flocks of birds (lost count when a flock flew over a tractor). I take the next exit and pull into a plaza that looks exactly like the last one. But the towns are too far from the tollway, and I don't want to pay tolls yet. Still, pulling up to the generic gas pump gives me an eerie feeling, like we've been driving in circles, passing this same pump, and we'll never get out of Kansas.

Gas is a penny more than it was four hours ago, but I have no choice. I fill the tank and head into the convenience store to pay the outrageous pump price.

When I come back with two Coke Classics, Jake's standing beside the car, stomping his foot and shaking his leg. "Yee-haw!" I shout, ignoring the truckers who turn and stare. "Country music finally got to you?" I hand him a Coke.

"Thanks, Matt." He takes a swig that empties half of the 20-ouncer. "You didn't have to get that fill-up. I would have been driving out here on my own and paid gas."

I give him a look designed to wither. "50-50, Jackson. Want me to keep driving? I'm not tired, except of Kansas."

"Nope. 50-50, Mays."

Jake takes over and gets us out of Kansas and into Colorado.

We drive all day, changing drivers every couple hours, usually at rest stops, where we race to the water fountain or run around the car to loosen up. The time goes pretty fast, considering we're spending it inside a rusty, overloaded piece of metal.

On my last Colorado shift the sun hangs above the horizon, directly ahead of us, making it hard to see the road in the white glare. We use the sun visors. We've worn out the air conditioning, and I'm not sure if it's hotter with the windows open or closed. Jake's been testy for the last 50 miles.

"Okay, Jake, would you rather—"

"No way," he rudely interrupts. "I'm not playing your stupid *druthers* game."

"Yes, you are," I reply sweetly.

"Forget it, Matt." He's so crabby it makes me want to laugh.

"Would you rather stick your arm into a barrel of snakes or a barrel of rats?" I ask.

"I'm not playing."

"Then the answer is both." Emma and I have made him play this game with us a hundred times.

He huffs. "Are the snakes poisonous?"

"No."

"Then snakes."

"There. Was that so hard?" I keep it up until he fires *druthers* back at me. We pass through Colorado, with Jake choosing to jump from the roof of a two-story house, ride a lion, and tread water for 12 hours. I opt to eat nothing but cheese for the rest of my life, swim in a pool of ketchup, and marry the king of England.

A car passes on the left, and a little boy peers out the back window at us. I wave at him and make a funny face. Mountains frame us on three sides. It's hard for me to take them in.

They're almost too beautiful, sending shadows down the surrounding hills.

"I've seen more of America in the past 14 hours than I have in the last 17 years," I comment, glancing at Jake. His profile shows his broad chin and intense eyes. I'm worried about how he's going to handle all the attention he's going to get as a varsity player at a major university. "Jake, let me ask you something."

"I thought we were done with that game." He sticks half a Snickers in his mouth.

"This isn't a game." I'm remembering Emma's question to me last night. "What do you want out of college?"

"What do I want out of it? How about—to get there?"

"I'm serious, Jake. What do you want?"

"A double cheeseburger and fries?"

I frown over at him. "And I'd kill for a hot shower. But that's not what I'm asking, and you know it."

"All right. Let's see. What do I want out of college? Fun." He reaches over and fiddles with the AC controls. It's an avoidance tactic because, for the first time all day, it's not sweltering hot in the car.

"What else besides fun?" I press. "You could have stayed in Hamilton and had fun."

"You're not going to let up, are you, Matt?" He sighs. "Uh— play hoops."

"Maybe. But you haven't said much about basketball since you made the team. "

He reaches behind his neck and jerks his head to one side. Something cracks. "You don't miss much, do you, Matt? I don't know. After I made the cut, I had a little trouble getting into it. Nothing's ever as great as you think it's going to be."

I smile to myself, thinking about how Emma and I have watched Jake get disillusioned with marathoning, biking, astronomy, playing the guitar, tennis.

"What? What are you smiling at?" Jake sounds irritated.

"I was just remembering what Emma said—that Jake Jackson has the Penultimate Plague."

"Penultimate? I don't get it."

"Okay. What is it you love about basketball, Jake?"

"Chicks in the stands screaming my name?"

"Very funny. I'm serious. Think about it. Is it sinking the ball? Scoring? I don't think so. For some guys, it's all about winning. But not for you."

He unties his shoes and kicks them off. "I don't like losing."

"Do you know when I see you light up on the court?" I picture Jake at his last game, shooting his final free throw. "You live for that second before the ball falls into the net—or bounces out. That millisecond when it can still go one way or the other. That's the Penultimate Moment."

Jake doesn't move. Finally he shakes his head and grins. "Man, I love that—that second before it drops. It's better than the swish of nothing but net."

"Penultimate Plague," I say.

We drive in silence as color drains from the sky, leaving us with our own reflections on the dark windows.

Jake takes over for the last stretch of Colorado. He puts on a Coltrane CD, and I manage to snooze for an hour, curled up in a ball with Jake's jacket over me.

I wake up when the car bounces over potholes. I figure Jake must be exiting for gas again, but this doesn't feel like a plaza. For some reason I don't sit up or let on that I'm awake. It's like the atmosphere inside the car has changed. It's charged with an excitement coming from Jake. I know he's up to something.

The hum of the highway stops, and tires crunch gravel. Peeping through my window, I see that the only light comes from our headlights and a million stars.

Jake steps on the accelerator, and the car surges. Gears groan, as if the Ford is trying to give birth to an SUV. The buzz of the road spins to a whir. Colorado blurs in my window. I have never felt this much speed.

"Yes," Jake whispers. "100. 105. 110."

The car vibrates, but it feels like we're skimming the road. It rattles so loud I picture bolts popping out and bouncing on the road behind us.

Then, as quickly as it came, the rush subsides. Speed evaporates, like air seeping from tires.

I let out my breath. "Good."

"Matt?" Jake sounds startled.

I sit up and stare at him. His face is flushed."If I'd wanted to fly to L.A., I would have employed the services of an airplane, Jake."

"Witty, even in her sleep," he observes.

"So how long have you been planning this little experiment in speed?"

"Travis said when he was out here in June, he got his old Chevy up to 100." Travis is one of Jake's white-water-rafting buddies. Jake grins at me and looks about 12. "I hit 115." He pats the dashboard.

"And was it worth risking your life and that of your sister's best friend?"

He shrugs and acts like he's thinking it over. "At the time."

"That's just it, you idiot. For a fraction of a second, right? Penultimate strikes again. Emma's right." We bounce along in the dark, our headlights shooting dusty lines of light in front of us. "All I can say is that it's a good thing your sister isn't along for this ride."

"No kidding," Jake agrees. "Emma's idea of reckless driving is holding the wheel at 10 and 2:30."

I want to stay angry with him because he's always doing stupid things like this. But I can't help smiling at the thought of Emma in a car going 115 m.p.h.

"Pull over," I command. "My turn."

Eight hours later I'm floating in a sea of more automobiles than I have ever seen. Los Angeles, California, is one gigantic car lot. I was driving on the 605, Jake snoring beside me, with sun filling the car and bright flowers lining the highway, when all of a sudden somebody turned the *on* switch. Cars streamed onto the wide freeway, as if they were feeding into a river.

I feel as if I'm driving in a video game at the Cameron Arcade. Cars merge in and out of lanes all around us at the speed of light.

A tiny red convertible zips inches in front of us. I slam on the brakes and sound the horn.

Jake jerks himself awake, smashing his head on the ceiling. "Ow! What's—?" He stops, mouth open, and squints at the ocean of cars. "Where did they come from?"

"Everywhere." I roll down my window and let in hot wind and angry honks.

Jake fumbles with the glove compartment. The map, along with half the contents of the compartment, falls to the floor.

"Come on, Jake. Where are we?"

Jake peers out the window as a semi bullies its way in front of us. "I don't know, Matt." There's panic in his voice. "But we're not in Kansas anymore."

7

Jake holds up a fistful of crumpled maps. "Matt, I can't read road maps! You know that."

I do know that. And he's even worse when it comes to asking for directions. It's a wonder he ever gets anywhere he's going.

I turn on the car's flashers.

"Matt, what are you doing?"

Slowly I pump the brakes until the Ford comes to a complete stop in the middle of the freeway. "If you can't read the map, then I guess it's up to me," I say calmly.

A solid chorus of horns wails at us. I smile at the drivers as I unhook my seat belt.

"Matt," Jake stammers, "you can't—"

But I can't hear the rest because the horns are too loud. "Better take off your seat belt," I shout. I motion for him to swap seats.

He's so flustered, it takes him three tries to get loose. It's not easy for six-foot-three-inches of guy to maneuver over the console and into the driver's seat. He looks so frantic, I can't help laughing.

People give us the finger and shout obscenities as they pull around our stalled car. It strikes me as surreal, and I laugh harder. I can't stop laughing.

"You're crazy, Matt." He turns off the flashers and forces his way back into the line of cars while I ferret through junk on the floor and find the right map.

"Now we're in business." I smooth out the crumpled California map. Turning it over for Los Angeles, I spot the blue snaky line labeled 60. "Exit there!"

"Now? There are two lanes to get over."

"Unless you want me to take the wheel again," I suggest, fingering my seat belt.

"Never mind. I got it." He turns on his signal and eases right.

I wave at the drivers he cuts off. They don't return the wave. Once on 60, we pick up signs to Freedom University.

"I remember this," Jake says when we pass a row of what look like Southern mansions. "Frat houses. When I was here before, all the players got invited to parties in the fraternities."

In the next block the nonuniversity buildings look like they're part of another universe. Burned-out bricks are scrawled with graffiti. Boarded-up apartments line the weedy lots. On the corner an old man in torn, dirty pants and a T-shirt hunches over, as if he's dodging a rain shower. His gray hair is so long that it hangs over the cardboard sign hung around his neck—*Will work for food*. His eyes sink into his head, as if they've already seen too much.

I can't stand it. "Stop!"

"What? Here?"

"Pull over, Jake." I rifle through our lunch bags and come up with four granola bars and a bottle of Gatorade.

"Don't, Matt," Jake pleads. "Not here."

"I'll just be a minute. He's so skinny, Jake." I have my seat belt off and the door open before the car rolls to a stop.

I have to run back half a block. When I get close, the man frowns and takes a step back. He's probably afraid I'm going to hurt him.

"Hello!" I call, walking the rest of the way. "I'm Mattie Mays."

"Albert Sanchez." He nods slightly.

I hold out the granola bars. "I'm sorry. We ate the apples and plums. Do you like granola bars?"

He holds out his hand, and I pass them over, setting the Gatorade at his feet.

"This is my first time in California. I'm starting school at Freedom University."

"My son is starting school. In Nicaragua." Albert's eyes open wider and let out light when he mentions his son.

"You must be so proud," I say.

He smiles, showing yellow, decayed teeth, and then rips open the chocolate-chip granola bar, Jake's favorite.

"Matt, we have to go!" Jake calls, backing the car up to us.

I introduce them. "This is Albert Sanchez, Jake. Mr. Sanchez, this is Jake Jackson. I guess we have to go now. It was nice to meet you. Maybe I'll see you again down here. At least I'll know somebody in L.A."

"I thank you for these." He waves the granola bars at us while I climb back into the car.

"Only you, Matt." Jake shakes his head as he pulls away from the curb. "Only you."

It takes us another half hour to find my dorm because Jake refuses to follow directions, claiming he remembers where it is. I don't mind. The campus amazes me, with its green lawns and ivory statues. All of the buildings look like libraries, except for what's going on in front of them. Guys are playing Frisbee. Girls are sunbathing right out in front of everybody. Other students are carrying boxes and refrigerators and suitcases.

"You could fit a dozen Hamiltons on this campus, Jake."

He laughs. "Yeah, but who would want that? Okay. There's my dorm. I don't think yours is that far from mine."

Ahead of us a brick building rises above fat-leaved trees. A white sign with black letters announces *Gillette Hall*.

"Jake, that's my dorm!" The lawn is crawling with students and parents, who are carrying loads from their cars. "At least we're not the only ones moving in on Sunday." We skipped freshman orientation. Jake claimed he didn't need it, since he got oriented while he was out for basketball. I needed the extra days at work, even though it would have been good to get here sooner than the day before classes start. It might take me that long to find the classrooms.

Jake finds an illegal parking spot in front of Gillette Hall, and we get out, grabbing a load.

"Home sweet home," Jake says, juggling a box of books.

"As long as there's a shower, I will love it." I can't explain how it feels to be on the verge of moving in here. I'm guessing that for most students, they're thrilled at the new burst of independence. I don't feel that. I've pretty much been on my own for as long as I can remember. I'm moving from a mostly empty apartment house to an overflowing dorm, from a single room to a shared one.

I have to wait in line and register to get my room key. Then I talk Jake into taking the stairs to the fourth floor—no easy task since he's carrying a crate of my books. There are as many guys as girls in the stairwell, and they all act like they know each other already. They even act like they know Jake, nodding or saying hi to him as we dodge past.

An extremely cute guy comes trotting down the steps and nearly runs me over. "Hey!" He smiles at me, and I automatically glance away. But I think I'm smiling, a little. I look up, and he's gone.

Music blares at us as we stroll up the hall. It's dueling guitars, with rap coming from the other end of the floor. We find room 444. I stand in front of the door, my door. It already has a white erase board with *Welcome Gillian and Matilda* written on it.

"Great start," I mutter, erasing the last half of my name and adding what I need to spell *Mattie*.

I hold out the key, look back at Jake, then knock.

"Matt, you don't have to knock on your own door."

A voice from inside calls, "Come on in!"

I seem to be paralyzed, so Jake shifts the box he's carrying and reaches around me to open the door.

A girl looks up from her desk. She has one of the most beautiful faces I've ever seen, high forehead and perfect skin. She's African-American, taller than I am, maybe five foot eight. She's wearing a tie-dyed shirt and fringed jeans, and there's a peace-sign poster above the desk. She smiles. "You Matilda?"

"No. Well, yes. Mattie."

"Well, that's a relief. Shut up here with a white girl named Matilda might have been a little much." She smiles, showing perfect teeth. "I'm Gillian. Not Jill, though."

I reach out to shake her hand, and the duffel bag I'm carrying drops on my foot. "Sorry."

"*Your* foot," she says, shaking my hand. "Nothing to be sorry to me about." Her fingers are long and strong, and I know mine are sticky. If I smell half as bad as Jake does from our road trip, Gillian is probably already planning to switch roommates. "Well, welcome to your room." She sweeps her arm like a game-show hostess. "Beds were bunked when I got here, so I left them that way. We can take them down if you don't like sleeping on a top bunk."

I peer around the room, which is smaller than I'd pictured it. Two desks, with the unclaimed one under the only window in the room, two dressers, two tiny closets, a small fridge, a TV, and bunks against one wall. The walls appear to be pastel green cement. "I've never slept in a bunk bed," I admit. "Sounds like fun."

Gillian laughs. "Fun? Girl, you need to get out more. Where did you say you're from?"

"Missouri."

"Uh-huh.".

Jake shoves past me to the empty desk and dumps my crate of books there. "I'm Jake. And these are getting pretty heavy. I'll run down for another load."

As soon as Jake leaves, Gillian says, "Very nice. Boyfriend?"

It takes me a second to get it. "Oh. Jake? No. Friend." I feel like I should say something else, maybe ask about *her* boyfriend. But I don't know what to say. "I'd better go help unload stuff."

I run down the stairs, kicking myself for not being friendlier. I want to be. I just don't know what to say. College may be a fresh start, but I'm afraid I'm still the same old Mattie.

It doesn't take many trips to unload my things. After the last load, I walk Jake to the car. All I want to do is take a shower and then e-mail Emma about the whole trip.

"Are you sure you don't want me to help you unload, Jake?" I'm barefoot, and I can't remember taking off my shoes. But it feels good to have the grass under my toes.

"That's okay, Matt. The other guys have probably moved in already. They can help." He points across the quad, where the tower of Jones Hall rises. "That's where I'll be, if you need me."

"You know, tomorrow is Monday," I say, remembering our promise to send Emma a postcard every Monday. "You think Emma will be looking for a postcard the first week?"

Jake doesn't answer.

I look up at him and see that he's not listening to me. His face has a stunned expression, like he's witnessing an explosion.

"Jake?"

"Who is that?" he whispers, but it doesn't sound like he's asking *me*.

I follow his glazed stare to a tall, blonde female, lean and tan, in white shorts and a white T. Her perfectly straight hair barely moves as she strides across the lawn toward Gillette Hall.

"Earth to Jake." I wave my hand in front of his face. I've seen Jake like this before. He is a guy cliché. "Jake, snap out of it!"

"Matt, did you see her? It's like she's everything beautiful about California, all rolled into one. She looks like an angel."

The *angel* is gone, but Jake's still staring after her.

"A California angel?" I feel like I've stepped into a cartoon. Jake's eyeballs should be on springs, and the caption would read, *Boing!*

Jake turns to me and puts his hands on my shoulders. "Mattie, she's in *your* dorm. You have to introduce me to her."

"Tell me this isn't another Jake Jackson's love at first sight."

"This is different, Matt."

"So was Amy. And Allyson . . . and Autumn . . . and that's just the As."

"Okay, okay. I may have fallen for a few girls in the past—"

"A *few* girls?"

"But this is different. I'm serious, Matt. There's something about her."

"Hmm . . . couldn't be that she's beautiful, could it?"

"You wouldn't understand."

"Ouch."

"Be serious, Matt. You have to find out who she is, where she goes—everything you can about her. Please? I need you, Matt. I have to meet that girl. I think I just discovered the answer to your question—what do I want out of college? I want that girl!"

8

Monday morning I drag myself out of bed early, even though my first class isn't until noon. I'm a little nervous about starting my work-study job in the English department. "You sure I look okay, Gillian?" I try to smooth down my rebellious hair.

"We should all look so okay," she says. "Now go! Can't be late on your first day."

I hustle out of the door, feeling as if maybe I really am on the verge of making a fresh start, a new life for myself. Here in California, on this campus, I'm just Mattie Mays, student. Nobody knows anything else about me, unless I choose to tell them.

I'm halfway down the hall when I hear a familiar voice. "Why, Trevor, you are just too kind!"

The voice catches me off guard. It's like the sound is out of context. So my mind can't wrap itself around the words, and I can't identify the speaker.

"Matilda Mays? Who would have thought? I heard you were coming here, but I absolutely did not believe it until I saw it with my own two eyes."

My spine tingles, as if it's freezing, or thawing, as the realization spreads through my vertebrae. *Valerie*. I turn to see Valerie Ramsey on the arm of some jock sporting a football jersey. Her auburn hair is longer than when I last saw her, which was right after graduation, and right after she'd broken up with Jake . . . again.

"Hey, Val," I call up the hall. She hates "Val" as much as I hate "Matilda." Fair's fair.

Tugging her football jock with her, she moves down the hall toward me. "I cannot believe they put you in my dorm." She says it with her homecoming-queen smile.

"And here I thought it was *Gillette* Hall." I couch my sarcasm with a fake smile. I don't have time for this. On my list of the Top 10 People I Do Not Want to See Today, Val Ramsey is #3, right behind Osama bin Laden and that guy who played Ernest in those stupid Ernest movies. If Val makes me late on my first day, I'll personally force-feed her chocolate cake until she gains the "freshman 15" and the abundant zits she so richly deserves.

"You always did have that unique sense of humor," Val observes, not smiling at it. She turns to the jock. "Trevor, this is Matilda Mays. I knew her and her mother back home." She turns back to me, her thin lips pressed together, pausing, probably to make sure I didn't miss the "and her mother" part. "Trevor is a sophomore. He's on the football team," she continues proudly, squeezing his arm, as if to make sure Trevor is real.

I can't help myself. "So you were on the team last year?"

"I played varsity." His pride matches Val's. A his-and-hers set. Cute.

"Must have been hard to blow the last game of the season like that." Driving through Kansas, Jake had told me all about the loss to the bottom-ranked Tigers to end a nine-game winning streak. "Guess you underestimated the competition, huh?"

Trevor stands up taller and puffs out his chest. "No sir! We didn't underestimate anybody. They just turned out to be a lot better than we thought."

My tongue aches because I'm biting it so hard to keep from

laughing. This is fun, but I have a real job to go to. "Well, nice to meet you, Trevor. I gotta jet."

Val and I forget to say bye to each other as I take off down the hall, wondering why they would put the only two girls from Hamilton, Missouri, in the same dorm, on the same floor.

I knew her and her mother back home.

Valerie Ramsey does not know me or my mother. She thinks I'm ashamed of Mom, but I'm not. I wish I could get her to stop drinking, but I'm not ashamed of her. I love her. And she's worth at least a hundred Vals.

But I still don't need Val broadcasting my family problems.

I jog the rest of the way to the Edgar building, where the English department lives. The school's college bulletin said the building was named after somebody who died with more money than the entire state of Missouri. They worded it differently.

I take the stairs—not that I'm an *ele-phobe* or anything. I just like the exercise opportunity afforded by eight double-stairwells. Right. Besides, everybody knows that elevator inspections are almost always out-of-date or forged by the mafia.

I exit onto a blue-carpeted hall, banked on both sides by see-through offices, separated by pretend walls. I've still got 10 minutes to find the right office. A phone is ringing off the hook, which is a stupid expression to think because there are no hooks. I pass the doorway of the office with the ringing phone. On the door it says *Admissions Office.*

The phone won't quit. I picture some poor kid on the other end of the line, feeling total rejection. Not only will she never get into Freedom University, but now she has to suffer the indignation that they refused even to answer her calls at the admissions office.

I can't take it anymore. I do an about-face and step inside the office. I snatch up the receiver. "Good morning! Freedom University admissions. How *are* you?" I sit casually on the edge of the desk and smile at the spectacled woman frowning at me from her cubby across the narrow aisle. "How may I help you?" I ask sweetly into the phone.

"Oh, good. I thought I had the wrong number." The voice sounds older, maybe a mom's, relieved now.

"I'm so sorry," I say. "Minor emergency. Nothing to worry about. Terribly sorry to keep you waiting, though." My British accent is creeping back.

"I was wondering. . . ." The woman hesitates. "Well, I'm not sure who to talk to. The thing is, my son really wants to attend Freedom University next year. But his GPA misses the requirement by two-tenths of a percentile. He's working hard this semester. He had a bad freshman year, you see."

She cares so much. I can feel the strain over the phone. The love too. I feel guilty being here—not in this office, I mean, but in this school. This woman wants her son here so desperately. I'm not sure my mom even knows the full name of this school. And I know she'd be much happier if I went full-time at Curtis Café and stayed in Hamilton.

The real admissions secretary still hasn't appeared.

"Listen," I say, "you tell your son to keep working hard. Then you write the admissions office and tell them . . ." I glance at the frowning, spectacled woman's desk and steal her first name while she's pretending to ignore me. I lower my voice. "Tell them Eloise in admissions promised that your son would get special consideration because of his recent scholastic efforts. Tell them Eloise promised."

"Do you mean it?" she asks, as if I've given her a gift.

"I'm not sure if it will do any good, to be honest. But, blimey, it's sure worth a try, don't you think?"

"Well, yes." She sounds a little confused. "I do think so. And thank you. Thank you so much, Eloise."

"Say, it does me good to hear from a mum who cares so much. Better push off now. Ta-ta."

I hang up fast. A woman in a striped pantsuit is heading my way. "Have a good one," I tell the real Eloise as I make my exit.

I stroll down two more halls and find the English department. Before entering, I tug on the hem of my skirt. I own exactly one skirt, and I'm wearing it—a straight black pencil, very businesslike, but short enough to let me look my age. My short-sleeved top is loose enough to look professional, and my sandals have heels. I slip off the backpack and wish it were a briefcase.

Opting not to knock, I open the door to the English offices and stride on in. "Morning," I announce to no one in particular.

Three men in suits are huddling by wooden wall mailboxes. They stop talking, turn, nod, and continue.

"As you were." I approach the big desk in the center of the alcove. Halls extend from three sides, corridors lined with offices. I sense that I'm in the eye of the English hurricane. Emma would love this.

"May I help you?" asks Mrs. Nancy Colton. At least, that's who she is if she's at her own desk. The nameplate even includes "Mrs."

I reach over the desk to shake her hand. "Mattie Mays, the new work-study assistant for the English department."

She shakes my hand, then stands up quickly and grabs her purse. "I'm sorry . . . Mattie, is it? I hate to abandon you on your first day. But one of our former colleagues passed away. Her memorial service is—" she consults her watch— "in 20 minutes. I'd really like to be there."

"Not a problem." I drop my pack behind the desk and move around to the now-empty chair.

"Simply answer the phones. Take messages. I should be back before you leave." She straightens the pens on the desk. "Oh, and if you have to"—here, she drops an octave—"go to the ladies' room, the phone will ring over to the dean's secretary. She can take the call."

"Great." I smile at her. "Don't worry about anything, Mrs. Colton."

"Well, all right then. I'll show you around the offices next time, if that's all right."

"Go." I smile at her as I take her chair.

People come and go, not seeming to notice that I'm not Mrs. Colton. I can pick out the profs who have been here since the beginning of time—not by their gray hair, but by their clothes, which they haven't replaced in a couple of decades. Two jackets have corduroy patches on the elbows.

But they're not all clichés of English profs. A woman in her early 30s—"pleasingly plump," Em would call her—walks in. She smiles like she's managed to sneak Snickers bars out of her file cabinet without being seen. She's wearing a denim wraparound skirt and a pink shirt, which is only a shade pinker than her rosy face. Her hair hangs in a long, brown braid down her back.

"Hi." She reaches across the desk to shake my hand. *Her* hand sports a diamond ring. "Christina Wolynski. You're new, right?"

"Mattie Mays, brand-new assistant."

"Well, don't let these stodgy old profs scare you off." She says it so loud, obviously on purpose, that the remaining two profs by the mailboxes turn around.

"Who's stodgy?" asks the tall, skinny man, who—now that he's smiling—looks like an old Jimmy Stewart on downers.

She winks at me. Then she pulls out a stack of papers from her mailbox and disappears down the south hall.

The office clears. I lean back in the chair.

When the phone rings, I jump. "Hello? Um—I mean, English department."

"This is Eric. The VCR isn't in room 112!"

"I'm sorry. This is the student assistant. Mrs. Colton had to leave. You need a VCR?"

"No kidding! I desperately need a VCR. I'm the grad assistant. I'm supposed to teach this class for Dr. Frost. He said he had a VCR all lined up and a film he wanted them to see. They'll be here in five minutes!" His voice gets higher as he gets more panicked. "How am I supposed to teach the class without a VCR?"

I think about telling him that pushing the *On* button of the VCR isn't exactly teaching the class. But it doesn't seem like the right time—a fact that has rarely stopped me in the past. Em and Jake would be proud. "No problem," I say at last. "Do you have the tape?"

"Yeah. But what good is that if—"

"I'll get you a VCR." I hang up and call the operator. In less than a minute, I'm convincing the media center that I'm Mrs.

Colton, and the media personnel are in big trouble for not sending the VCR. They promise to get a machine to room 112 in five minutes.

I get up and start to look for room 112 so I can deliver the good news to Eric, the panicked grad assistant. Truth is, I'd like to get a look at him, since, in spite of his lapse in cool, the guy could still be boyfriend material. I like the idea of falling in love with an English grad assistant.

The phone rings again.

I keep going. I really want to check this guy out.

But the phone keeps ringing. I can't stand ringing phones. I lunge back to the desk and grab the receiver. "Hello?"

"Mrs. Colton?" a crackly male voice asks. Probably a smoker, by the raspy sound of his breath. I will never understand voluntarily inhaling charred tobacco.

"I'm sorry. Mrs. Colton had to step out for the morning. This is Mattie Mays, student assistant. Could I take a message?"

"This is Dr. Weaver. I'm going to have to cancel my 10 o'clock freshman comp class. Would you go in and tell them we'll start on Wednesday instead? You can let them go after that."

"No problem," I say, wondering if there's a more professional response. I try again. "I'll be happy to take care of that for you, Dr. Weaver."

He hangs up before I can ask him for the room number of the class to be freed. College is great. No subs. If the teacher misses, so do the students. Fair is fair.

I rifle through Nancy's desk, careful not to disturb the perfectly aligned index cards, the neat pile of paper clips, or the sharpened pencils. Finally I come up with a course catalog. There are four Weavers teaching at the university. But only one of them has a freshman composition class at 10 o'clock, Monday-Wednesday-Friday.

I snatch up a notebook and pen, just to look more official, and leave in search of room 303.

I hear the class before I actually see the number on the open door. 303. These people are noisier than middle-school kids with a substitute. I take a deep breath, hug my notebook to my chest, and walk in. It's the rear entrance, and I find myself behind the back row of a small theater room. Wood fold-down seats descend on an incline, sloping toward the teacher's desk at the bottom. Blackboards cover the wall behind the desk.

I have to make my way down the aisle to get to the front of the class. Long-legged freshmen guys slowly pull back their stretched-out legs and let me pass.

Someone in a row I pass whistles. A wolf whistle. It causes an eruption of laughter, then murmurs and a couple of agreeing whistles.

I am beyond embarrassed as I make my way down the steps, my head held high. What are these *boys* doing at a university? They're adolescent. If this is what I have to choose from for a boyfriend, I will remain single the rest of my life.

9

I've almost made it through the maze and down the aisle to the front of the classroom when someone calls out behind me, "Hey, baby! Here's an empty chair!"

"Forget that!" cries another voice as I reach the first row. "Here's an empty knee, gorgeous!"

The guy who says this should quit school and pose for *Macho Magazine*. He's athletic, without being *jock*. Thick black hair surrounds a broad forehead and chiseled face, not unlike a face one might expect to find attached to a Greek god.

None of this matters, however, since he's the most obnoxious person I've ever met. I glare at him, and he actually pats his knee.

That does it. I stride to the front of the room and set down my notebook on the tall black desk that's more suited for a chemistry experiment than a book of poetry.

Students turn to each other and laugh. They break into private conversations as, wishing I'd been born a foot taller, I assume a position of authority at the mountainous desk.

I stare at them, my gaze moving slowly from right to left across the crowd. I mow them down, one by one. Finally a silence envelops the room. Even Greek God has stopped flirting with the redhead next to him.

"This is a university class?" I ask, my English accent sharp and on the money. "Right, then." I'm not angry, merely perplexed. "Not the lower levels?"

"It's freshman comp," offers the sullen redhead, leaning into obnoxious Greek God.

"Is it? Fabulous." Turning my back on the room, which feels a bit suicidal, I walk to the board and pray I'll find a piece of chalk there. The big green board takes up the whole front wall, below a rolled screen.

I find a stub of white chalk and scrawl on the board *Professor M. Weaver*. I underline it with a flair and plunk down the chalk. The plunk echoes in the now-silent room.

I wheel around as if I'm Mary Poppins. "I am Professor Weaver. We shall be spending this hour together all semester."

Whispers punctuate my audience.

"Oh, man!"

"We're done for."

"Yes!"

"No way!"

"Cool."

Greek God sinks into his chair, no doubt envisioning his first English grade.

"Oddly enough, the subject of our introductory discussion, and your first essay—750 words by Wednesday—is 'My Ideal Woman or Man...and How to Properly Treat Her or Him.'"

Groans pepper the room, then die down.

"As this is your first assignment—and given the fact that we appear to have a remedial class—let me give you a hint, shall I? Catcalls, wolf whistles, schoolyard banter, and other bits from the scrappy lads should not appear in this essay, unless they exist as part of an apology."

Greek God straightens in his chair. "Let me be the first to apologize."

"That seems only fitting," I say, not giving an inch.

He grins, leans toward Sullen Redhead, and whispers something that makes her giggle.

"You there. Mr.—?" I narrow my eyes at him until he supplies his name.

"Me?" He straightens himself from the redhead. "Vandermere. Carson Vandermere."

"Brilliant. Mr. Vandermere, perhaps you could help me sort this out. Are we dealing with *epistemophobia* or *ergophobia* in your case?"

He wrinkles his broad brow at me. I try not to notice that he's every bit as cute with his brow wrinkled. "Come again?" he requests.

"Oh, dear. Simpler language? I'm asking if your problem is a fear of knowledge, *epistemophobia*—or merely a fear of work, *ergophobia*."

"Careful, Carson!" hollers some guy two rows behind him.

"Can you talk slower?" asks Sullen Redhead. "Your accent is kind of hard to understand, you know?"

"My *English* accent?" I clarify.

She shrugs. "Yeah. I mean, like, *English English*, you know?"

"Like, you know?" I pronounce every consonant and vowel, unlike S.R., Sullen Redhead. "I will do my best to reduce your *anglophobia*, especially as this is an English class."

"Angle-what?" *Her* forehead does not look good wrinkled in wonder.

"*Anglophobia*," I answer. "Fear of England and all things British."

"Whatever," she murmurs.

Greek God—Carson Vandermere—stands and delivers a short bow. "I humbly apologize for my inappropriate behavior. And I will work hard to overcome any personal fear of knowledge and hard work. I just have one problem with this assignment." He takes his seat again. His timing is impeccable. I'll give him that. "I have already met my ideal woman—five foot six, amazing black hair, blue eyes, awesome English accent. Would personal interviews be acceptable?"

The peanut gallery chuckles.

I smile, as I might to a wayward schoolboy. "Presumably your unimaginative description was intended to have some resemblance to me?"

He nods.

"As lovely as the prospect of interacting socially with you is, Mr. Vandermere, I must decline." Not even *he* could miss the sarcasm. "I, myself, suffer from *lyssophobia*, the fear of becoming mad."

Sympathetic *oohs* and *ouches* travel through the crowd.

I like being an English teacher from England. Somehow it's much easier than being a college freshman from Missouri.

I turn my attention to the whole class and start our discussion.

The hour flies by, with half the class offering their versions of the ideal man or woman.

"The ideal woman *has* to be a redhead," insists S.R. in the front row. "You guys want someone fun, and redheads—not blondes—*do* have more fun."

"Ah, but do they know it?" I ask.

I try not to get in the way of the conversation that explodes around the room like fireworks, or gunshots. For the most part the answers sound pretty well thought out. I'm surprised. The words *soul mate* come up too often, and the phrase "be there for me." But most people claim they're looking for someone they can trust, someone they can talk with and be themselves around. I try to remember the decent answers, in case Jake and I are ever stuck without a Love Rule for Emma's postcard.

There are exceptions to the general wisdom of the class. "Enough with the love crap," claims a guy wearing a football jersey with the number zero on it. "My ideal woman has to want to have sex as soon as she meets me."

The class snickers.

"With *you*, presumably?" I query.

Students give in to all-out laughter.

"And you are—? No." I hold up my hand to stop him from

speaking. "Do not answer that, please. I would rather not know your name. Nameless, you have just validated my inherent mistrust of strangers."

Carson Vandermere doesn't say anything the rest of the class period, although he's definitely paying attention. He stares at me the entire time.

When I see class time is about over, I walk up the aisle, returning the way I came. I haven't dismissed the class, and I think they're anticipating some grand finale from me. They watch silently as I make my way to the back door and walk out.

As soon as I'm out, I dash to the nearest corridor, then race to the English office before "my" students figure out that class is over.

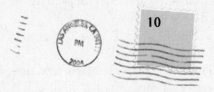

That night I meet Jake by the Freedom University Flying Squirrel, like we planned. I remembered to stop by the campus bookstore right before it closed. The girl at the register was ready to go home, so I didn't have much time to browse for postcards. I ended up with a picture of the campus. Pretty boring, except it does show the giant statue of the Flying Squirrel, Freedom's mascot. And the legend explains the tradition of rubbing the squirrel's nose for good luck.

I arrive at the Squirrel five minutes before midnight, even though I know Jake will probably be late. I'm surprised by how busy the campus is at this hour. Few people are alone, though. Three couples are stretched out on blankets on the quad's perimeter. One of the couples is really going at it. The others are talking and looking up at the stars, which are scarce and dim compared to Hamilton skies. I can't even see the Little Dipper or Cassiopeia.

I try to imagine Emma looking up at this exact moment and both of us seeing the same Big Dipper. I think I feel my first pang of homesickness.

A guy who's so cute that he doesn't look like he needs luck

walks up to me, or rather to the Flying Squirrel. He nods, then rubs the squirrel's nose and strolls off. The statue itself is about four feet long. The nose has been rubbed so often that the outer brass and another layer of some kind of metal have worn through to the black cast. I wonder if that means Freedom students are very lucky or that they've needed a lot of luck over the years.

"Matt!" Jake comes jogging out of the darkness and into the relative light of the quad. He waves and looks happy to see me, so I forgive him for being late. For Em's sake.

He reaches out and rubs the squirrel's nose. "I stopped by the bookstore for a postcard, but they're closed."

I pull out the card I got. "It's not great. Maybe next time we can go somewhere and get a cool one."

Jake squints up at the spotlight above the squirrel. "Let's get out of here. I feel like I'm on stage."

I follow him to a vending area behind his dorm, and he gets us both Milky Ways, the best candy bar in the world. We sit down, the only ones at the dimly lit table.

"I don't know what we're supposed to write for Emma," Jake complains, unwrapping his candy. "We've only been here a day."

"Yeah. But it was the longest day in history, don't you think?"

He laughs. "I tried all afternoon to get a line on that girl."

"Which girl? Wonder Blonde?"

"Matt," he scolds. He looks so pitiful that I feel like scruffing the top of his head, but I restrain myself. "You've got to find out about her. It shouldn't be that hard. Just be on the lookout. You're bound to see her again and—"

"I saw her tonight." I say it before I've thought it through. What I saw isn't going to make Jake feel any better. His Wonder Blonde and some tall, dark, and handsome were kissing good night in front of the dorm when I left on the postcard hunt. It was quite a show actually.

"You saw her?" Jake stops chewing caramel. "When? How was she?"

"Pretty much like yesterday, Jake," I say.

"Didn't you introduce yourself? You *knew* I wanted to meet

her. How could you just walk past her? ignore her?" He's getting fired up now.

"Jake, she was . . . occupied."

"Occupied? What are you saying?"

"Well, I think she was finishing up a date or something." He looks like I slapped him. "Or not."

"She was with somebody?"

I nod. "Maybe it was no big deal, Jake."

He sighs. "Of course she'd have a boyfriend. A girl like that?"

We sit there for a minute while two girls get Diet Cokes out of the machine, then leave, eyeing Jake over their shoulders. Then they join up with two guys and walk off.

I'm thinking Jake might be right about the cool people already being paired off with each other. Like Gillian. She's really cute, and she's got a great boyfriend. She told me all about Michael, the engineering major at MIT. What if all the good ones are already taken?

Suddenly I'm so tired I can hardly keep my eyes open.

I set down the postcard. Pale light falls on the picture of Freedom University's lucky Flying Squirrel. Luck. Jake and I are both going to need a lot of it. "Come on, Jake. We can't let Emma down. I'll start."

I pull out my pen, which I've learned to carry in my pocket with my keys, since almost nobody carries a purse around here. I address the postcard to Emma. Then in big letters, I print *LOVE RULE #1*.

"So," I coax, "what's our first word of wisdom on love?"

Jake heaves another sigh. "Love, huh?" He takes the pen out of my hand and turns the card to face him. I read upside down as he writes, *The chances of finding love at this university are slim to none.*

Without a word, I take back pen and postcard and scrawl beneath Jake's line, *And Slim went home.*

FREEDOM UNIVERSITY home of the LUCKY FLYING SQUIRRELS

LOVE RULE #1

The chances of finding love at
this university are slim to none.

And slim went home.

Emma Jackson
RR 1
Hamilton, Missouri 64644

11

By Wednesday afternoon of my first week of university life, I'm beat. Working 20 hours a week and carrying 18 hours of classes is tougher than I figured. Might have something to do with the fact that I still can't sleep at night.

After my last class I drag myself to the fourth floor of my dorm. In the stairwell I have to pass by a couple pressed up into the corner of the third landing, kissing as if they're on the iceberg-battered Titanic. I excuse myself as I brush past them, but they don't seem to notice.

I quit digging for my key when I hear Gillian's Dave Matthews Band CD. I open the door to laughter that's louder than the music. Gillian has company. Again. She's a great roommate, and I know I really lucked out in the roommate department— already the dorm is filled with roommate horror stories. It's just that she's *so* nice and so much fun that she attracts people to our room night and day.

Gillian greets me as soon as I walk in. "Hey! How's our very own Professor Weaver?"

"Say what?" asks a girl I haven't met yet. She and Gillian could be sisters, except she's not as thin as Gillian. And her clothes look a lot more expensive—tall leather boots, leather skirt, form-fitting white shirt. Gillian's wardrobe is more colorful—baggy jeans with a retro Nehru shirt and a feather necklace.

Gillian introduces us. "Mattie, this is T.C. T.C., Mattie Mays, my roommate. Mattie's been impersonating an English professor."

"Why?" T.C. obviously doesn't approve of me already.

"So, did they have their essays done?" Gillian asks.

Naomi and Laura, our suite mates, scoot apart so I can climb to my bunk, for lack of another square foot of space to sit. Gillian's books are scattered on my bedspread, and I have to shove them over. "I'll probably never know. The *real* Professor Weaver's back."

"Is he cute?" Naomi asks. Her shiny black hair is twisted on top of her head with a clip, and she's wearing more makeup than my mom on bar nights. But on her delicate face, it works. Naomi may look Japanese, but she's 100 percent American—fourth generation, I think. So far I haven't heard her talk about anything except men, a subject on which she claims expertise.

"Prof Weaver? Cute? I guess, if you're into 75-year-old asthmatics," I reply.

Gillian laughs. "Did he find out what you did? Did you get in trouble?"

I shrug. "Yes. And kind of. I guess it wasn't that hard to figure out I was the one who taught his class. He came by the English department after *his* class and gave me a warning." He'd tried to act severe, but he and Mrs. Colton both looked like they were about to crack up laughing. Still, it was pretty embarrassing.

Naomi, obviously disappointed in my description of Professor Weaver, turns to Laura, her roommate. "So go on, Laura. Keep telling us about the new love of your life."

Clearly this is the conversation I've interrupted. I feel sorry for Laura. I think she's cute—blondish hair, average figure. But next to Naomi, who's head-turning striking, Laura seems to wilt. As she talks, Laura never quite makes eye contact. Her hand hovers around her mouth, as if she's prepared to trap the wrong words if they slip out.

"I didn't say he's the love of my life," Laura objects, her cheeks getting blotchy pink. "But he *is* very good-looking, and he sounds smart in Intro to Business. I caught his name today, when the prof did roll call. He's last—Steve Zeller."

I lean back on my bunk, then pull out a candy wrapper from under my head. The wrapper isn't mine. "Well, I don't think I'd ever marry a Zeller," I offer. "I'm not sure I could handle being last."

"She doesn't want to marry the guy," Naomi protests. "You'll settle for a date, right?"

"A date would be great," Laura says softly.

"Does he like rhyme?" I ask, repeating *a date would be great* twice in my head. They don't get it.

"You are so lucky you got Naomi for a roommate!" exclaims Naomi. "Consider yourself enrolled in 'How to Get a Date 101.'"

"How about transferring to 'How to Get 101 Dates?'" I suggest.

They ignore me, although Gillian grins up at me. I've never been good at making friends with girls. Em is the exception.

Naomi fires a set of questions at Laura. "Is he a freshman? Native Californian? How tan is he? Is he quiet or a clown? Does he volunteer info in class, or try not to be seen? Does he take notes or doodle?"

I'm amazed to watch how systematic Naomi is about this.

Finally, when Laura has done her best to answer at least two dozen pertinent questions, Naomi stops talking and tries to pace, which in a room the approximate size of a cereal box proves impossible. Her spike-heeled sandals click on our bare floor. Gillian's right. We need a rug.

"All right. Not studious. You can't ask him if you can copy his notes or if he heard when the test is going to be." Naomi sounds like she's thinking aloud.

"That's right," T.C. chimes in.

"He sounds like a poser," Naomi continues, "possibly a player in high school. He'd never fall for the dropped pencil or book trick. Calling him about *anything* presents too great a risk."

"Good. Because I don't think I *could* call him," Laura admits.

"You have to get him to notice you," Naomi concludes.

"How do I do that?" Laura asks. "Plastic surgery or breast implants?"

"Laura!" Gillian scolds. "You are gorgeous already!"

Naomi grins as if she holds the secrets of the universe. "We have our ways."

"Such as?" T.C. challenges.

I'm staying out of it.

"Scent," Naomi answers. "Men are oblivious to our power over the olfactory sense."

I'm impressed that she's used *oblivious* and *olfactory* in the same sentence. I sit up and pay attention now. I may audit "How to Get a Date 101."

"I have perfume," Laura offers. "Is that what you mean? Should I wear it to class?"

"Not just any perfume," Naomi corrects. "We want to *trigger* the right senses. Leave that to me." She goes on to assign wardrobe and hairstyle. Then she cautions, "But, my dear roomie, even though we will be coaching *you* and making *you* over, you must never forget what this relationship is really about."

We're silent, waiting. The music plays in the background.

"This relationship," Naomi says, "is all about *him*. You must be consumed with *him*."

"Not a problem." Laura laughs weakly. "I can't think about anything else."

"No, no, no!" Naomi cries. "He can never know that you *want* him. Only that you think he's funny. And smart. And interesting."

"Oh, I do!" Laura insists.

"But it's all in the way you *show* it. You must demonstrate your high opinion of him, without ever leading him to believe that you're *interested* in him."

"How?" Laura whines.

"This should be good." T.C. pushes aside my books and sits on my desk.

"Laugh loudest at his jokes," Naomi instructs. "Stare intently at him as he talks and answers questions. Nod emphatically, showing your total agreement with whatever he says. Second his comments in class whenever you can. 'You know, Professor, I have to agree with that last comment. That puts the whole thing into perspective for me.'"

If there's this much intrigue and finesse to relationships, no wonder I haven't had many of them. I should be taking notes. "Why couldn't she just ask him if he wants to go get something to eat after class?"

Naomi looks at me as if I've suggested Laura go to class dressed as a vampire. "Come on, Laura." She leads Laura back to their room, as if protecting the girl from me. "We are about to launch 'Operation Steve.'"

After they leave, I lie back down on my bunk, suddenly missing Em so much I could cry.

12

Gillian invites me to go eat in the cafeteria with her and T.C., but I can tell T.C. wants me to say no, so I do.

As soon as they're gone, I log on to my e-mail, hoping there will be something from Emma. She and I send lots of short e-mails, but neither of us lives online the way most students here seem to.

I have a string of e-mails waiting. Two want to sell me online pharmaceuticals. One offers to enlarge a part of my anatomy which, as a female, I don't possess. And there's one from Emma. I click on it.

```
:: Dear Mattie ::
I can't wait to hear the sequel to Professor
Weaver's saga. Wish I could have seen you
giving those guys what they deserve! Have you
seen any of them around campus? There must be
scores of cute guys (like Greek God) to fall in
love with. Be careful! Talk to God about them,
Mattie.
```

My senior year started today. My locker has the exact same tinny, chocolate smell last year's locker had. Can you believe it? Classes feel all wrong without you. Nobody knows sign the way you do. I didn't realize how much people depended on you to translate for me. Don't worry about it though. Ms. Leedy is assigned as my "tutor," and she's pretty good at signing. Guess who came up to me at our first game and asked about you—Dennis! Did he even go to games when he was in school? At first, when I saw him across the field, I thought he was his dad. I hope he changes his mind about college.

BTW, what's up with Jake? He hasn't answered my e-mails since Monday. Is he still hung up on Wonder Blonde, or has he moved on already?

Speaking of "moving on," sorry Val's in your dorm. Have you run into her again?

Gotta jet.

Love you! Miss you! Emma

P.S. LOVE RULES!

I hit *Reply*.

Sorry—no sequel to Prof Weaver. The real Prof Weaver stood up. I do admit I've had my eye out for G.G. (Greek God), aka Carson Vandermere. But he's vanished. Still haven't met Eric, the grad assistant, the one I rescued by VCR (Get it? VCR, CPR? Nobody here gets my humor).

Tell Dennis hi for me next time you see him.

Don't worry about Jake. He's still in a fog over his Wonder Blonde.

You should be getting our first Love Rule, though—coming soon in a mailbox near you!

LYG (Love your guts), MM

Emma's e-mail does three things—

#1. It makes me feel guilty because I promised her I'd try to pray more once I got to college.

#2. It reminds me that I promised Jake I'd research Wonder Blonde for him.

#3. It renews the sick feeling in my stomach I get when I think of Val in my dorm. And that makes me want to follow through with #2 and investigate W.B. because anybody has to be better for Jake than Val.

I'm not totally without knowledge about WB. So far I know her room number, because I followed her from the parking lot to my floor. She's across the hall and all the way down. I know her name, Stella, because she and her roommate have a frilly sign on their door—*Stella & Amy's Place*. And I heard her call, "Amy! Wait up!" as she chased after her roommate this morning. She wasn't shouting her own name, so she's not Amy. That leaves "Stella." In addition to these details, I heard elevator music coming from her room. That tells me a little more than I care to know. Still, she has to be better than Val.

I have a feeling Jake will expect more W.B. facts than I've gathered, so I log off e-mail and stroll down the hall to *Stella & Amy's Place*. It's barely 5:30, but the dorm feels empty. It's weird. When 4:30 rolls around here, it feels like dinnertime. At home, if our parents had tried to make us eat this early, we would have advised them to go ahead and buy white belts and white shoes, take up golf and shuffleboard, and make the move to Florida.

I decide to take my chances and knock on Stella's door, hoping that I'll come up with a reason for my visit, if she's actually home. It occurs to me that if I were visiting Stella because I wanted to be her friend or to meet new people, I'd be terrified. But as Private Eye Mays, I'm fearless.

The door opens a crack, and Stella peers out. She rubs her eyes, like she's been sleeping, but her long blonde hair is straight and perfect. She squints at me. "Hi."

"I'm sorry. Did I wake you?" I can see behind her that the light is off, shades are drawn, and she's alone. "You're not Amy."

"Amy? She's my roommate." She opens the door wider and flips on the light. "Amy has lab until eight."

More luck than any PI has a right to expect. I step in when she leaves the door open. "I'm really sorry if I got you up."

"That's okay." She peers in the mirror and smoothes down the back of her hair, although I can't see one hair out of place. "I never took naps at home. But I can't seem to help myself here."

I take in the room as she sits on the bed by the window. There are three Disney movie posters on one wall, the wall I instinctively take to be hers. Stuffed bears and turtles cover her bed. Above her desk—it has to be hers—little glass turtles line the sides of her bookshelf. Greek letters are stuck on both mirrors. I don't see any regular books, only textbooks and a dictionary. No fun reading. Also, no clothes on the floor or on chairs.

"I think Amy has a class I was considering adding," I lie. "I wanted to ask her about her prof." I'm still standing, waiting to be invited to sit.

"Boy, I don't have any idea what she's taking. We haven't talked much about our classes," Stella admits.

I smile. "I'm Mattie, by the way. Mattie Mays. I'm on the floor."

"I thought I'd seen you around." She yawns again. "Stella Robinson. Hey, if you want to check out that class, Amy's class schedule is on her desk."

I cross the room and look at the schedule, wishing I could see Stella's. "What's your major?" I ask Stella. It's a dumb line, one I've been asked approximately 20 dozen times in three days. Usually guys ask it and then kind of tune out when I answer that I'm major-ing in firearms, or cockroach study, or nuclear war.

"My *major*?" She says it as if I've accused her of having an affair with a military officer. Then her shoulders sag. "Your guess is as good as mine. I don't like math or science, and I'm not crazy about English either. I do like my logic class, so far. But I don't know if you can major in that. I've got logic at eight o'clock, Tuesdays and Thursdays, and I don't even think I'll mind getting up for it."

"Who's your prof?" I ask.

"Nettles. I got off to a good start with him, I think." She checks her watch.

I can take a hint. "Well, I better jet. I'll catch Amy later." I move toward the door. "Again, sorry I woke you up."

"Don't be." She gets up and walks me to the door. "All I do is sleep."

"And I haven't had a good sleep since I've been here."

Stella laughs. It's a nice enough laugh. "It was nice to meet you, Mattie. I'll tell Amy you stopped by."

"Thanks again. Guess I'll see you around."

The door closes behind me. At least Private Eye Mays will have something to tell Jake. And except for the turtle obsession, I didn't turn up anything too horrible.

13

I thought my dorm was noisy until I walk up the sidewalk to Jake's dorm. Rap and alternative boom from open windows. Guys are yelling at each other. A shirtless stud in a ponytail shouts out the window at two girls strolling up the sidewalk.

This is college—the part they don't put in those brochures they send you and your parents.

I stand outside and stare up at Jones Hall, a gray stone building that looks older than Gillette. A man in overalls, a mop bucket in each hand, staggers up the walk, slightly dragging his right leg.

A football comes flying, heading straight at him. I lunge for it and make the catch, a second before it hits.

Two guys tackle each other to the ground, laughing. One of them scrambles up and yells, "Nice catch! Toss it here!"

"Watch where you throw this thing, huh?" I fire back a perfect spiral. Jake says I should have been a quarterback.

"Thanks for that," says the man with the mop.

"No problem." I stick out my hand. "I'm Mattie."

"Bob."

He has a nice smile, and I'm thinking he's maybe 60 or 70, but it's hard to tell.

"You live in Jones?"

I shake my head. I'm still getting used to the fact that most of the dorms are coed, although in Gillette Hall, girls get even floors and boys get odd, which I take as metaphor.

Bob and I talk for a while about how things have changed at Freedom over the 30 years he's worked there. Turns out he's married to June, the woman who cleans Gillette.

"I know your wife," I explain, as we both walk into Jones. "A couple of nights ago, when I couldn't sleep, I met her in the lobby. She told me to drink warm milk and sleep with my toes pointed in at each other."

Bob's face softens. "That sounds like my Junie."

Before we head off in different directions, Bob gives me some insider advice. "Use the two washers on the outside of the row in the laundry room, and stick with the big dryer in the middle, if you can. And if your meal plan runs out by Sunday, try the cafe on Tarragon and 14th Street. Good prices . . . but stay away from the chili."

I take the stairs to the eighth floor, stopping on the landing between six and seven because a guy in boxers is running down, barefooted. The cement smells like stale beer and vomit.

Jake's room is farthest from the stairwell. Not good in case of fires. I step over potato chip bags, a basketball, five or six books, a freshman, and a laundry basket before I reach Jake's door. He opens it after the second knock.

"Mattie?" Jake's wearing shorts, sandals, and a surfer shirt. He already looks totally college and completely California.

"Yep. Here I am. Now, what were your other two wishes?" It's funny seeing him here, like we're both out of context, like we've been playing college, but now we'll have to go back home for supper. "So, you going to invite me in, or are you denying all things Missouri?"

Jake steps back, grinning, and whispers, "Come in, but keep it down. My roommate finally dropped off to sleep. He's been driving me crazy."

"Did you lose in the roommate gene pool?" I whisper back. His room is bigger than mine—maybe twice as big, with two more windows. They've fit a reclining chair under one window, plus a fridge, a big TV, and a huge entertainment console. Makes me feel like I'm visiting from the slums.

"My roommate's okay." Jake motions for me to sit at his desk. He pulls up the other chair, lifting it so it won't squeak. "But he won't stop talking about this gorgeous teacher he's fallen madly in love with. Then she quit or was kidnapped or something. He kept me up all night moaning. Swears he will never stop looking for her. It's getting to me. I'd just as soon he slept through Sunday."

"Ick. A teacher crush?" I try to sneak a look at him, but all I see is a lump wrapped in a spread.

"So, did you find out anything about *her?*" Jake's not wasting any time.

"Yeah. But first, Emma asked me why you haven't been answering your e-mails. Write her back, Jake."

"Okay, okay. I will. Now, what about *her*, you know, the blonde?"

"You mean Stella?" I pretend not to notice that he's salivating for information.

"Stella? Is that her name?"

For the next few minutes, I make him pull the information out of me, piece by piece. True, I don't have that much info, but I like to make the most of what I've got.

"Greek letters, huh?" he says, when I remember the part about Greek letters on the mirror. "She must be in a sorority. I've been hanging out at the ATO house a lot. They're talking to me about pledging."

"Do you have time for that, Jake?" It's what Emma would ask if she were here. "How's basketball going?"

He shrugs, and I get a bad feeling. "It's okay. Go on. What else about *Stella?*" He pronounces her name as if it's a magic word.

I've saved the best for last. "I managed to find out a little about her classes."

"Matt, you got her schedule?"

"Not exactly. But she did confide that she's got logic at eight on Tuesdays and Thursdays, with Professor Nettles."

"Logic? *I* could take logic. I'm only carrying 12 hours—Coach's dumb idea."

"I don't know, Jake. I've known moths who were more logical than you."

He ignores the slam. "So what else did you learn about *her?*"

I know he wants to hear about her boyfriend, or whoever she was kissing outside the dorm. But my investigation didn't get that far. "What else? I mentioned the turtle fetish, right?"

A groan sounds from the lump on the bed. Jake and I have gradually worked out of our whispers.

"Hey, dude," says the lump, without rolling over so I can see him, "I must really have it bad. I was dreaming about her. I even thought I heard her voice. But she didn't have her English accent."

"Her . . . English accent?" I repeat. I'm getting a crazy idea. But it couldn't be. Because I don't believe in coincidences. It's ridiculous. There must be dozens of teachers with English accents at this school, right?

"Um, I need to go eat before the cafeteria closes," I whisper.

"There! That's it. I heard her, Jake!" The lump on the bed rolls over.

I see the black hair first. Then those big brown eyes of a Greek god.

He sits up so fast he bumps his head on the wall. "It's *you!*"

I hop to my feet and plan the quickest getaway route. The window's out—eight stories. I'd have to ease past Jake to get to the door.

"Carson?" Jake sounds confused. "Take it easy. What are you talking about? What do you mean 'It's you'?"

"There!" Greek God points to me. "How did you do it? How did you find her, dude?"

I edge toward the door, willing myself invisible.

Jake narrows his eyes. He's starting to get the picture. "Matt?"

"Where have you been? Why weren't you in class?" Carson is on his feet now, stepping closer to me. He's taller than I remembered. And better looking. "This old dude showed up and claimed *he* was Professor Weaver! What were you—?" He stops a foot from me and eyes me from head to foot. "I thought I'd never see you again, Professor Weaver."

I try to smile. "Well, you never know, do you? Crazy thing, life."

His brow wrinkles, and again I can't help but notice that he's still cute, wrinkled brow and all. "Your accent. What happened to it?"

"Mattie Mays, what did you do?" Jake smoothes back his hair, a gesture I've seen too often right before a Jake-explosion.

"Matt? Mattie Mays?" Carson asks Jake. "Is that her name? Wait a minute. You're not saying this is *your* Matt. From back home? I thought you were talking about a guy!"

Jake manages to totally ignore his roommate and stay focused on me. "Matt, you impersonated an English professor with an English accent?"

I try a little laugh. "Funny, huh? English—English?"

Jake glares at me. If he were a cartoon, his face would be red and there would be steam spouting from his nostrils.

"So arrest me for impersonating an English prof. I didn't plan it, Jake. It just happened. You should have been there. Your pal here and the others were so obnoxious—"

"We were!" Carson agrees, jumping to my defense.

"—that I thought they should be taught a lesson," I continue.

"And she was great at it too, dude," Carson adds. "Best class any of us has had yet. We all did that essay."

"Matt! Carson stayed up all night writing that essay of yours."

"The other Professor Weaver wouldn't even collect them," Carson explains.

I turn to Carson. "He wouldn't? Why not?"

He grins and shakes his head. "He's not near the teacher you were."

"Oh, puh-leeze!" Jake begs. "Matt, this isn't Hamilton. You can't go around impersonating people whenever you feel like it."

Now *I'm* getting upset because the last thing I need is a lecture from Mr. I'm-madly-in-love-with-a-blonde-I've-never-met Jackson. "Look, the only reason I came over here was to deliver my espionage report on your Wonder Blonde."

"Don't bring Stella into this," Jake snaps.

"Stella?" I grab the doorknob because if I don't leave in 30 seconds, I'll undoubtedly throw something. "I'm going to dinner."

"I'll come with you!" Carson calls.

"You already ate!" Jake barks.

Carson shoots him a glare. "What's it to you, dude?"

"Yeah, *dude?*" I second.

I whip open the door and make my exit. Turning around I holler, "We're still on for Monday at midnight! I'll come here."

"I'll be here," Jake fires back, as if we've agreed to meet at high noon and bring our six-shooters.

I wheel around and storm down the hall.

Behind me I hear footsteps. "Wait! Mattie! Wait for me!"

I slow down. Greek God, Carson Vandermere, is running after me. My heart feels like a hand is squeezing it. Greek God wants to have dinner with me. *Me.*

I think I am about to have my first college date.

Greek God

Man, I have dreamed of being alone with this babe since the first minute I saw her. And dude, make no mistake about it. I'm making this one—professor or no professor—mine. Carson Vandermere doesn't take no for an answer. She's not getting away again.

"Wait up, Prof—Mattie!" I book it down the hall after her.

She slows a little, enough to let me catch her. I take my time. I like this view. She is so hot. Hair and body of a goddess. The way she carries herself—this chick has style and confidence. Make no mistake about it.

The football jocks huddled by the stairwell stop talking when she walks by. Heads turn. I don't think she even notices.

She jerks open the door to the stairs.

"Mattie, there's an elevator this way!" I run up to her.

She keeps going. Her footsteps echo in the empty stairwell. I take a deep breath and head down after her.

"I'm begging you to wait up, Professor!" I know she's not really a professor. When the real prof showed up, we figured she was a grad assistant, trying to teach us a lesson. But she will always be Professor Weaver to me. "Professor Weaver!"

That stops her. She turns and frowns up at me. "Don't call me that."

Her nose crinkles, and she's so cute angry that I'd like to jump her right here on the stairs. I think even Amy, the girl I left back home, would understand.

"Sorry. Mattie." I hurry down the flight of stairs to catch up with her. "Can't we walk together?"

"Are you really going to the cafeteria?"

Her eyes are the bluest eyes I've ever seen.

"Dude, I'm starving," I lie. I'd just had the mystery meat, mashed potatoes and gravy, and a chocolate sundae. But I would eat worms for five minutes alone with this babe.

She starts down the stairs again. She must be an exercise fanatic or a nature freak or something. I can live with that.

We walk across the commons, even though the grass is wet from the sprinklers. A vision flashes through my head—Prof and me tumbling to the grass, rolling over and over in the mud.

"Yo! Carson!"

I nod to Jeff, one of the ATOs. Showing with a hot chick like this has to bump me up a notch on the cool scale. Always room at the top.

I manage to step in front of Mattie and open the door for her.

"Thanks," she says, passing in front of me. Her hair smells like raspberries and spring. Dude, I want her.

She leads the way to the cafeteria line, which is long, too long, especially since hardly anybody's here, compared to earlier, when I had the mystery meat. Mattie takes a tray and hands me one.

"I'll bet you're a vegetarian," I comment.

She frowns at me. "Why would you bet that?"

"Hey, I'm not saying there's anything wrong with it. I mostly eat vegetables myself." It's a lie, but all's fair in love.

"I'm getting a burger," she announces, gliding to the grill section.

I tag after her. "Yeah. Me too."

We're standing, waiting for the one lone server to leave the main dish line and come over to the grill. Normally I'd be shouting at the girl, a fat chick with a serious zit problem. But I can use the time to score points with Mattie.

"I have to admit, Mattie," I begin, giving her my full-court grin, "I really had you pegged for a vegetarian."

She looks at me as if I've accused her of only eating people.

I laugh. "I just mean you seem like someone who loves animals . . . and well, maybe wouldn't want to eat them." I'm good. What chick doesn't like animals?

"Of course I love animals. I don't eat dogs. Or cats. The animals I do eat are meant to be eaten. Why else would they be made of meat?"

I can't tell if she's serious or kidding, but I don't laugh. Worse to laugh at the wrong time than to *not* laugh at the right time, I think. "Totally," I agree. "But a lot of hot, sexy babes try to tell me red meat is bad for me."

She raises her eyebrows. "No. Fuzzy, green meat is bad for you."

"What do you want?" The fat, pimply girl in a white apron leans her chubby arms on the counter and acts as if we've been keeping *her* waiting.

"Two hamburgers," I order.

"And could I have the onions, lettuce, tomato, and pickles on the side please?" Mattie asks.

When we finally get our burgers, Mattie heads for a table by the window.

Two girls I met at the ATO kegger last night are leaving from a booth we pass. "Hey, Amanda," I call. Can't remember the other girl's name.

"Hey, Carson! Did you get over that hangover?" Amanda asks, laughing.

"Really, Carson," the other girl calls. She has auburn hair, and I remember meeting her at the party. I think her name is Veronica or Valerie. Something like that. "You were *too* much!"

She jerks her head in Mattie's direction and whispers, "What are you doing with *her*?"

I'm pretty sure I see a flash of jealousy in Mattie's eyes. That's a good sign. Chicks love it when a guy's a player. I wave to a brunette from my math class, a blonde from the dorm, and another girl I'm not sure I've met.

Mattie and I sit across from each other at a little table in the corner. She starts in on her brownie.

"You eat your brownie first?" I ask, making conversation.

She doesn't crack a smile. "Always eat dessert first. Life is so uncertain, don't you think?"

"Yeah. It really is," I agree.

She takes a drink of her milk. Iced milk, with ice cubes. "So what's your major, Carson? English?"

Once again, here I am at the threshold of the necessary boring conversation. All I want to do is get her by herself and make the moves on her. But a guy has to pay his dues. "English? Maybe." English is the last thing I'd major in, but I'm thinking it might be her thing.

"Really? An English major?" She widens those huge blue eyes at me, like I've said I'm majoring in pottery or cooking.

Maybe English isn't manly enough. "Right now I'm majoring in parties," I add.

"How's that working out for you?" she asks.

"Why don't you come and find out, dude? I could get you into some awesome frat parties."

She smiles and takes a bite of her burger.

I'll come back to the parties. I've planted the seed. Let her wait and hope.

"Did you grow up in California?" She shakes salt on her tomato.

"California all the way, dude! Wouldn't live anyplace else. We've got villas in Italy and France and a condo in Florida. But man, make no mistake about it. Give me California— surfing, tans, parties on the beach. Bet you're glad to be out of the Midwest, huh? Away from the cows and corn?" I throw down the rest of my dry hamburger. "This food bites. It all tastes the same. Next time we'll go out to eat. I'll take you to this new restaurant and bar. They know me there."

She bites into her burger as if it's a juicy steak. She is so sexy. "Mmmm. I really like the food here."

I laugh.

She doesn't.

I switch gears. "Well, food here is pretty good, most of the time. You're right." I bump the dialogue to safe ground. "So how long have you known Jake anyway?"

"Seventeen years."

"Almost your whole life, huh? Nice guy, Jake. Kind of out there, though. Like the way he had to parasail, even though you could see the storm moving in over the ocean."

Mattie frowns, and I'm afraid I'm killing the mood here. "What else is Jake doing crazy?"

"You ought to see him surf—how he waits for the big ones."

"He likes the risk."

I'm tired of talking about Jake. "Basketball's not *my* game," I admit. "Football all the way. I won all-conference in high school. I could have played college ball. They were recruiting me really hard. Not just this school either. I strung them all along. Those recruiting weekends were awesome. Parties like you never saw."

I entertain her with some of the best stories from my football career. Then I bring the conversation back to the ATO and Beta parties. I can tell she's really into it. "That's why I decided not to play college ball—might interfere with my social life, if you know what I mean." I flash her the crushing Carson smile.

Mattie glances over her shoulder at the cafeteria line. The line is the noisiest thing in the cafeteria, now that the room has mostly emptied. She's looked over there a couple times during our conversation. I'm wondering if she's thinking about getting something else to eat, but she's too shy to get it. Girls are like that—eat like birds when they're with you, then stuff themselves when you're gone.

"Could I get you something else?" I ask, after she's stared holes in the line.

She turns back around. "What? Oh. No. Thanks."

We're quiet for a minute. I think of another story about the time I ran for a touchdown against the Bulldogs. I'm about to launch into it, when Mattie interrupts my thoughts.

"So, do you have a job or anything?"

"A job? At school?" I laugh. I worked exactly four days in the summer. "No way. Even if I wanted to—and don't get me wrong. I don't—I wouldn't have time. Not with the ATOs and the Betas rushing me so hard. You know, I could get your buddy Jake into a frat, I think."

"Jake? You really think he wants to join a fraternity?"

"Why wouldn't he? They've got parties every night. I don't even remember last weekend. That's how tanked I got. Sunday, I was so sick—"

"Sounds like fun," she says.

"You got that right." I figure I've left her hanging long enough. "So, how about I let you see one of the frat parties up close and personal?"

Instead of answering, she peers again over at the cafeteria line. I follow her gaze and see that a small riot is starting. The pimply fat girl can't get food out fast enough.

Mattie stands up. "Excuse me, Carson."

I stand up too. "More dessert? I'll come with you. I can get you through that line faster."

She's already walking toward the little crowd of angry, hungry latecomers.

I jog past her and get there first. Carson Vandermere takes control. "Hey! You!" I shout at the fat girl. "Get a fresh brownie out here now! A big one!" I turn to smile at Mattie.

The fat girl doesn't budge.

"Now, dude! I can get you fired, you—"

I feel Mattie's grip on my arm. "Carson!"

I put my hand over hers as she squeezes my arm. "It's okay, Mattie."

She takes a deep breath. "Listen. I can see that you've set

aside this special time to humiliate yourself in public. I'll leave you to it then."

And just like that, she walks away.

"Mattie?" I watch her as she goes to the end of the cafeteria line. Then she ducks under the counter bar and comes out on the other side, the serving side of the counter.

"Mattie, what are you doing?" I shout over the crowd of students, who have stopped clamoring for food and are watching us.

"Hey!" barks the fat girl to Mattie. "You can't come back here."

Mattie takes an apron off a hook and slips it over her head. Then she pulls plastic gloves out of a Kleenex box and sticks them on. Stepping beside the fat girl, she addresses the cafeteria line. "Please to follow in line. We will take next person now." I think her accent is Swedish, but it could be Polish, one of those languages that sound Russian.

Hearing her talk like this—exotic, foreign—turns me on.

People shuffle themselves into an orderly line, and the first girl tells Mattie she wants a chicken sandwich. Mattie serves the next two people, and eventually the fat girl nods and moves to the deli line.

I'm not sure what to do. "Mattie!" I wave at her.

The crowd turns. Mattie looks up from the hot dog she's making.

"I-I guess I'll go back now. I'll call you. Great getting to know you."

"Bye, bye, Carson," she hollers back in that accent. She hands a hot dog to a guy who's as skinny as the dog. "I will always cherish the initial misconceptions I had about you."

I smile. I'm not sure what she means, but I can't take the crowd staring. "Cool. Later."

Back at the dorm, as I ride the elevator back to the eighth floor, I take stock of my first "date" with Mattie Mays. I made a great impression. The problem will be waiting the required three days to call her. I'm not kidding myself. Things could have gone better. I'm still not sure why she bailed on me at the end. And I didn't get her sense of humor. But maybe Jake can help prep me for next time.

'Cause make no mistake about it, dude. There *will* be a next time.

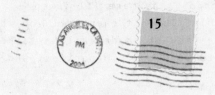

15

Mattie

:: From: mattmays@free-u.edu ::

:: To: emmaj@missouri.net ::

:: Subject: Date #1 ::
Em, how can a guy who looks so much like Mr.
Right turn out to be so Mr. Wrong? I just had
my first college date with none other than
Greek God from my English class. And get this—
he's Jake's roommate! I won't go into detail,
but we sorted it out and went to dinner in the
school cafeteria—just Carson Vandermere III and
yours truly.

Date #1 REPORT
He was . . .

1. BORING—Em, I should have brought along a

newspaper to read during dinner. The guy didn't get a single one-liner! Plus, he has severe allodoxaphobia (fear of opinions). I couldn't even argue with him because he was too busy agreeing with me. You know how I hate that. And hey—do I look like a vegetarian to you???

2. CONCEITED—Carson Vandermere III is so . . . so . . . California! I won't even tell you what he said about the Midwest, dude. All he talked about were his old buddies, old parties, and old girlfriends.

3. RUDE—The jerk flirted with every girl in that cafeteria. He even hit on our very own Val! Why do guys do that? And when did "hot" and "babe" become compliments? I should have thrown my hamburger in his face.

It's getting late. And I have an essay to write for English, a how-to paper. Maybe I should write "How to Pick Up Mr. Wrong."

Anyway, I had to share my disaster date with my best friend. Where did I go wrong, Em? Maybe he is too good-looking for his own good? Next time I'm choosing an ugly date, who can't possibly be this stuck on himself.

Disillusioned in dating, Mattie

P.S. I did meet a guy named Bob. But he's at least half a century older than I am and happily married to a nice lady. Sigh . . . Why

```
couldn't God put Carson's outsides on Bob's
insides?
```

Thursday morning I have an e-mail waiting from Emma.

```
Oh, Mattie, I got your postcard and your
First-Date e-mail on the same day. You poor
"babe"! Jake's not faring much better, huh?
Wish you were here and we could all escape for
a moon check.

Sorry, but I lol at Carson Vandermere. So much
for Greek gods in college clothing.

I'm expecting true wisdom from both of you in
the next Love Rule. I'm counting on you guys!
I've started a novel, so I need your research
more than ever.

Can't say I'm 100% behind your date-an-ugly-guy
campaign (How about an un-hot-guy campaign?).
But I know what you mean. Check out this verse,
Mattie—1 Samuel 16:7

Love, Em
```

Em strikes again. From time to time during middle school and high school, she'd toss out a verse, refusing to tell me what it said. She knew I'd have to go look it up, and that it was the only way I'd get into the Bible.

I scrounge in my tiny closet until I find the Bible Em gave me for my fifteenth birthday. The Bible is easier to find than the verse because it turns out there's more than one Samuel between these covers. Finally I locate the mystery verse, which is in the middle of a story about how David got picked as king, even though his older brothers looked the part and he didn't. Turns out young David looked so un-kingly that his own father didn't bother to call him in from tending sheep when Samuel came around to pick the next king. I have to wonder if "un-kingly" is something like "un-hot."

Em's verse is what God said to Samuel when Samuel was thinking David's older brother would fill the bill nicely. "But the Lord said to Samuel, 'Don't judge by his appearance or height, for I have rejected him. The Lord doesn't make decisions the way you do! People judge by outward appearance, but the Lord looks at a person's thoughts and intentions.'"

I smile to myself, wondering how Em does it, how she comes up with these verses that fit real life. Carson Vandermere definitely gets an A+ in outward appearance. Not sure what the *dude* scores on the inside.

The door bursts open, and in thunder Gillian and Naomi. Gillian's wearing red, white, and blue, with a flag kerchief triangled over her hair and red-and-blue striped sandals. Naomi is wearing a tan suede mini and a sleeveless cashmere sweater.

"Sweet!" Naomi exclaims, coming through the door first. "I told you. Operation Steve will not fail!"

"You're good, girl," Gillian says.

"Did I miss something?" I close the Bible, feeling kind of funny for having it open.

"Our little Laura has a date with Steve Zeller this weekend," Naomi announces. "She and I have a lot of work ahead of us. But we're one touchdown up." She does a little end-zone football victory dance.

"Congratulations. I should have hired you to coach me last night." I shake my head, trying to dump the cafeteria memories of Carson Vandermere III.

"Anytime, Mattie," Naomi offers seriously. "Is that a Bible?" She says it like you might question the presence of a dead rat.

I shrug. "My best friend back home, Emma, Jake's sister, gave it to me. Sometimes she sends me verses."

Naomi raises her eyebrows like I've been sticking pins in voodoo dolls.

"That's so cool!" Gillian slides into her desk chair. "Michael and I are both trying to read through the Bible this year."

"No kidding?" I ask, surprised. I haven't seen Gillian reading her Bible. But then again, our schedules are pretty opposite.

Gillian nods toward the big peace sign above her desk. "Peace, you know?"

I'm not sure I do know, but I nod.

"Now I get it." Naomi's lips tighten in a smirk. "That's why you and Mikey aren't doing the deed. You're scared you'll get sent to the fiery pit."

I don't know what to say. I kind of wish I could slip out of the room. Gillian and I have never talked about stuff like this. I admit I've wondered. She's totally in love with Michael. They IM for hours every day, and he calls her cell every night at nine on the nose because it's free minutes cell-to-cell. Almost everything Gillian has said about her high school years started with "Michael and I," so they had to spend every minute together.

Gillian laughs, not a nervous laugh but a warm, real one. "You don't get it, Naomi. Michael and I are waiting until we're married—even if we end up marrying other people. But it's not because we're scared."

"Okay," Naomi interrupts. "Because you're stupid?"

Gillian laughs again. "Because we're smart, girl! When we do have sex, we want to rock the house down—for the rest of our lives. God made the equipment, and God knows how to get the most out of it."

I'm probably blushing, but fortunately, it's like they don't even notice I'm still in the room. The only person I've ever really talked to about sex is Emma, and she's not having it until her wedding night—no discussion.

I've read my share of romance novels and watched enough movies to think Em is the exception. Everybody kind of assumes that if you've got a boyfriend, you're sleeping with him, especially in college. But who knows? I mean, if I believed all I read and saw in movies, I'd think everybody is skinny and gorgeous, and they all live happily ever after.

"Let's leave God out of this," Naomi begs.

"Never a great idea, but okay," Gillian concedes. "Even if I didn't have the user manual—the Bible—it makes sense to wait. I don't want to go leaving a piece of myself with every guy I date."

Naomi sighs and pulls the rubber band out of her ponytail, letting her shiny black hair loose. "And that's the difference between you and me. Now, I have bigger fish to fry." She walks to the connecting doors and calls, "Laura!"

The room feels awkward when she's gone. I put my Bible away. "That was pretty tight, Gillian." I think about how how much Emma would like her. Em says that intimacy without commitment is like icing with no cake. It's going to make you sick, sooner or later.

"Yeah?" Gillian sounds pleased. "Michael would have done better explaining. He's so ripped that people listen. I swear, that man could tell you blue is red, and you'd believe you'd been mistaken your whole life."

"I'd like to meet him."

"So what verse did your friend make you look up?" She settles in at her desk and turns on the study lamp.

"One about God not caring about the outside but looking at your insides—something like that." I throw my notebooks into my pack and try to think if I'm forgetting anything. "I told her I wanted to date an ugly guy so he wouldn't be all stuck on himself."

Gillian laughs again. Her laugh makes me think of waterfalls pounding over rocks. You can't help but smile. I can picture Gillian and Em together. I want to be like both of them when I grow up.

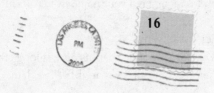

16

On the walk to Miller, where my history class meets, I think about Gillian and Michael, and I wonder what I'd do in their place, loving each other so much. But at the rate I'm going, I won't ever have to worry.

I get to Miller almost 15 minutes early because the "un-hot" guy I'm targeting is in my history class. I have him pegged as the kind of guy who rushes to show up 15 minutes early for everything. His name is Jeremy Skittles. For some reason, names stick with me. I remember most of the names of the kids in my classes after one or two roll calls.

I stop in the doorway of the classroom. Jeremy is the only one there, and he still looks nervous. Seated in the exact center of the front row, inches from Prof Brown's desk, he squirms in his chair and uses his index finger to slide his glasses farther up the bridge of his nose. Whoever named this guy was a prophet.

God doesn't look at the outside. I am *not* looking at Jeremy's bony, gawky, six-foot frame, or his uncombed, mousy hair. I am not noticing the white socks he's wearing with his penny loafers or the too-blue jeans that could stand up without him, or the block-striped shirt like 10-year-old boys used to wear. It's a good thing not to be a slave to fashion, right?

Instead of taking my seat in the middle of the classroom, I march directly to the front and ease into the seat next to Jeremy. "Hey, Jeremy."

He jumps, like I've startled him.

"I'm Mattie Mays. I remembered your name from roll call Tuesday."

He eyes me suspiciously. "Why?"

I shrug. I smile. Up close, I notice that his nose is long enough to be registered with the NRA, but his eyes are BBs. "So, Jere, where are you from?"

"Jeremy," he corrects, picking up his notebook and hugging it to his chest. "San Bernardino."

"Oooh, I heard it's beautiful there!"

"It's okay."

See? If this were Carson the Third, he'd be going on and on about his city.

"I'm a stranger in this land," I say. "Born and raised in Missouri."

"Huh." His lips don't quite come together, so three of his front teeth are in full view. He has good teeth. I'll bet he brushes after every meal. Thirty-two strokes per tooth.

"What are you majoring in?" I ask, trying to engage the inner man. "History?" It's a long shot, but I'm afraid he won't answer an open-ended question. I've given him a true-false.

"Physics and computer science, with a minor in molecular biology."

"Wow." A long and impressive answer. Eat your heart out, Greek gods everywhere. "Sounds like you really know what you want out of college."

"I'm sorry." He sets down his notebook and fingers the edges.

"Don't be sorry!" I object.

"Okay. Sorry."

A couple of girls walk in and plop in the back row. Then three guys sidle in and take the seats in front of them.

"Hey, Mattie!" calls Bryan. We sat together Tuesday, and he made some comment about how he thought he knew me from somewhere. He's way too cute to date. "Come on back," he urges.

I turn around and shrug. "Hey, Bryan." Then I turn back to my target. "You've got a great seat up here, Jeremy." Again I try to squeeze out conversation. It's about as hard as trying to get gossip out of Emma.

Jeremy starts to get up. "Here. Do you want my seat?"

I take his arm and pull him back down. "No! Sit down, Jeremy. We've both got great seats." True, it's a little weird. But I'll bet Carson Vandermere never gave anybody *his* seat.

Jeremy sits down, still clutching his notebook.

I'm getting jittery. Jeremy's nerves must be catching. I've never asked a guy for a date. Where's good ol' Naomi when I really need her? This is probably Lesson #1 in "How to Get a Date 101."

"Hey, Matt." Jake Jackson slides into the seat behind me. "What's with the front row seat?"

"Jake? What are you doing here?"

"I swapped sections."

I catch a glimpse of Jeremy. He looks like all the air has been siphoned out of him.

"Jake, this is Jeremy Skittles. Jeremy, Jake is an old *friend* from back home. The brother of my best friend, in fact."

Jeremy sits up straighter and nods at Jake.

With Jeremy taken care of, I turn back to Jake. "So why did you switch?"

"I had history at eight. To get into Stella's logic class, I had to take history at a different hour. You said you liked this prof, right?"

"Right. But logic, Jake? You actually signed up for logic, just because Stella's in there?"

He nods, but he doesn't look too happy about it.

"That's going pretty far, even for you, Jake."

"You should have talked me out of it, Matt. It was a dumb idea."

I think of at least a dozen one-liners. But he looks so sad, I save them. "Why? What happened?"

"The prof is a jerk. That's what happened. It was going all right. I got the seat next to Stella, introduced myself. She's really easy to talk to. Then *he* came in and started on me."

"Nettles?"

"He came in wearing these leather riding boots, Matt. Dressed in black. And he started hitting on Stella!"

"Come on, Jake. He did not."

"He *did*. You've seen Stella. And the guy's not that much older than we are, Matt. It's his first year teaching."

"So what's the deal? She likes him? You're jealous? What?"

"No, it's worse than that. He went out of his way the whole period to make me look like a fool. It worked too."

Again a dozen comebacks flash through my head, and I keep them to myself. Jake's not kidding around. And it's not like him to feel persecuted when he isn't.

"Thanks," he says.

"For what?"

"For swallowing those witty one-liners."

"Get out. Why would he pick on *you*, Jake?"

"Because he probably thought I was with Stella. Maybe he wants me out of the way. I don't know, Matt. But he wouldn't let up."

"What did he do?"

"He started asking me about the readings. I told him I just transferred in. But instead of asking somebody else, he kept throwing questions at me. What do I think of Hegel? Do I adhere to Aristotle more than Plato? What do I think of Bart and a bunch of other names I've never heard of? I felt like an idiot. Stella wouldn't even look at me. She rushed out after class."

Jake has been staring at his hands. He looks up and gets my full attention. "He reminds me of the way Ms. Magee used to hound *you*."

It's exactly what I was thinking as Jake was talking. Ms. Magee was the first English teacher I had after they made me skip a grade in high school. The woman acted like it was my fault I was in her class, and she made it her personal mission in life to tear me down and humiliate me whenever she could. Even thinking about it makes my stomach twist.

"I don't think he asked anybody a question except me, Matt. And when I tried to answer, he had this way of turning my words around, twisting them so they sounded stupid."

Jake is really hurting, and it makes my veins throb. "It will be okay, Jake," I promise, because I can't think of anything else to say.

"Yeah, right."

Professor Brown walks in. "Sorry I'm late." He smiles and strides to his desk. "Won't happen again—at least not *this* semester. My wife had a baby last night."

We congratulate him and ask all the usual questions—name, weight, and social security number.

The smile has become a permanent fixture on his face. "So, since I have a family to support, I better get down to teaching."

I've almost forgotten about Jeremy, who is armed and ready to take down every word that comes from the professor's mouth. I jot down my phone number and dorm room on a slip of paper and hand it to him. "Call me, Jeremy," I whisper.

He stares at the paper I've handed him. "Call you? Why?"

"Just . . . if you want to go out sometime," I answer.

He looks confused. "When?"

"This weekend?" I whisper.

For the rest of the class period Jeremy keeps pulling the paper out of his pocket, examining it, as if he suspects I've written it in disappearing ink.

17

When I get back to the dorm after my last class, Naomi, T.C., and Gillian are sitting on the floor, eating popcorn. I inhale the salty popcorn smell, and my mind flashes back to movie nights at Emma's.

I dump my backpack and wish I didn't have hours of homework to do this afternoon. "I just decided. I'm going to invent popcorn perfume. Make a million dollars and never do homework again." Without waiting to be invited, I steal a handful of the big-kernel variety.

T.C.'s staring at me, making me think I've dribbled butter down my chin or something. "Girl, do you always get this many phone messages?"

I laugh. "Me?" I've gotten exactly two phone calls since I've been at the university—one from Jake, prodding me to investigate his Wonder Blonde, and one wrong number, looking for Madeline somebody. I've called Mom twice, got her once. But I haven't heard from her and don't expect to, unless something's wrong.

"Well, today's your lucky day, Mattie," Gillian announces. "You have 11 phone messages—all male voices."

"You've got to be kidding." Maybe word has gotten out that the job of Mr. Right is available. Applications are coming from all over campus.

"I took three calls for you since I got here," T.C. complains. "All three were from Jeremy Spittles, or something like that."

"Skittles?" I only left him a few hours ago.

"Mmm-hmm," Gillian adds. "They're *all* from Jeremy Skittles."

"What kind of a name is Jeremy Skittles?" Naomi asks.

"Definitely not Greek," I answer, trying not to show how disappointed I am. Couldn't at least one be from someone else?

"Well, that boy needs to take my Dating 101 class. Multiple calls are a definite no-no. Gives the boy stalker status." Naomi takes a handful of the unpopped kernels from the bowl and nibbles them. I wonder if she knows they're called "old maids" where I come from.

Laura strolls in through our open connecting door. "I smell popcorn. Hey, Mattie." She pulls a slip of paper out of her shorts' pocket. "I took three messages for you."

"Don't tell me," T.C. pleads. "Jeremy Skittles?"

"How did you know?" Laura hands me the paper with Jeremy's name and number. "He wants you to call him back, if it's not too much trouble and if you want to and have time."

I sigh. "Guess I better call him back." I reach for the phone.

Laura snatches the receiver out of my hand. "Huh-uh! Me first. Naomi made me wait two whole hours to call Steve back. And my two hours are up."

"Steve?" I ask. "As in 'Operation Steve'? He called you?"

"Of course he called her," Naomi informs me, as if she'd scripted the whole thing.

"He asked me out for this weekend," Laura adds proudly.

"Where are you going?" T.C. asks.

Laura tilts her head. I think she's gotten her hair styled somewhere expensive. It looks good. "I don't know where we're going. Or when. Just that it's this weekend." She sighs. "And I would gladly go to the dentist with him, if that's where he wants to take me."

"Then by all means, be my guest." I bow and bequeath her phone rights.

"Thanks, Mattie."

Naomi checks her watch.

"Why did she have to wait for two hours?" Immediately I'm sorry I asked. Naomi rolls her eyes, as if bored that she has to put up with such ignorance. Then she runs through the Phone Rules of Dating 101.

"#1: Never call a guy first—unless you have a really good excuse.

"#2: Never call him right back. I prefer a two-day wait. I gave Laura a two-hour minimum because she was driving me crazy.

"#3: Remove from your vocabulary the four Ws and an H. Never ask him *where* he's going, *who* he's going with, *what* his plans are, *how* he's getting there, or *when* you'll see him. You couldn't care less.

"#4: When talking to him on the phone, be distracted. Have other people in the room.

"#5: Never ever remind him of anything, especially if it's about you.

"#6: Always end the conversation before he does."

I'm truly amazed. "Where do you come up with this stuff, Naomi?"

"Years of research," Naomi answers. "And you shouldn't call that Jerry Spittle guy either, although I'm not sure I have phone rules for a guy who calls a dozen times."

Laura is squeezing the phone so hard, it should turn to coal. "Now can I call?"

Finally Naomi gives the go-ahead. It's like letting a horse out of the starting gate. Laura punches in the apparently memorized numbers. While she waits for the pickup, she twists the phone cord around her fingers.

Naomi tosses Laura the Rubik's Cube from Gillian's desk. "Work on this while you talk to him. You'll sound less interested."

Laura obeys. "Hello? Steve? You said to call you back—Oh. Laura. Laura Kennedy. . . . Fine, thanks. How are you?"

She's silent, listening and twisting so long that it's agonizing to watch. I sit down next to Gillian. Emma would be praying, so I toss the call up to God, best I can. I'm not sure it's okay to pray that Laura gets her date with Steve. I mean, what if he turned out to be an axe murderer? So I just tell God to take it from here.

"Yeah. That's pretty funny." But Laura hasn't cracked a smile. I wonder what Naomi will have to say about this performance. "So, about this weekend? You know, you said you wanted to do something together this weekend?"

Naomi jumps to her feet and makes enough arm movements to land a fleet of bombers.

Laura, apparently aware of her breach of Phone Rules #3 and 5, shoots an *I'm-sorry-I couldn't-help-myself* look to her mentor. "Sunday? Um. Sure. What time?"

Naomi growls.

"Sure. Okay. Do you . . . Oh yeah. Better go then. See you Sunday. Bye, Steve." Laura hangs up slowly. If she were a cartoon, little hearts would be dancing from her head.

"Are you on with Super Steve?" Gillian asks.

I'm waiting for Naomi to explode. I scoot a little farther away from her.

"We're going out Sunday night," Laura announces.

"Sunday? Sunday!" Naomi repeats.

"That's what Steve said." Laura doesn't look worried. Not yet.

"'That's what Steve said,'" Naomi mimics, making it high-pitched and singsong. "You said he asked you out for the weekend!"

"He did," Laura returns. "Sunday?" She looks so hopeful. I can't stand it. It's like watching in slow motion as a kitten sits on a railroad track. I hear the train whistle.

"Sunday *is* officially part of the weekend," I try.

Naomi glares at me. I scoot closer to Gillian.

"Sunday is *not* a weekend date," Naomi insists. "You should have told him you were busy."

"But—" Laura begins.

Naomi shuts her down. "You played right into his hands." She taps her foot and seems to be talking to herself. "This Steve thinks he's a player, does he? Well, he's no match for Naomi. Think you can get away with a casual Sunday? Well, I've got news for you,

Stevie." She grins here and slowly lifts her gaze to the withering Laura. "Never mind, Laura. I love a good challenge. Operation Steve has just kicked up a notch. Your little Stevie is about to get more than he bargained for." She links her arm through Laura's and walks her back toward their room. "Come along, Laura. We have work to do."

When they're gone, Gillian says, "Your turn, Mattie." She hands me her notebook with the 11 messages from Jeremy, each one with his phone number. The first three numbers are different from the school exchange. Maybe Jeremy has his own place.

T.C. gets up, shaking her head. "I can't go through this again. You do what you got to do, girl." Then she leaves Gillian and me alone.

"Guess I better call him, huh?" I pick up the phone. "Just don't tell Naomi."

Jeremy answers on the first ring. "Hello?"

"Jeremy?"

"You called?" He sounds stunned.

"Well, *you* called. Right?"

"I'm sorry. But you said I could . . . if I wanted to do something."

I have to hold the phone away from my ear because he's talking so loud. "So you want to do something? When?"

Gillian laughs. If Naomi were here, *she* wouldn't.

"When?" Jeremy repeats. "This weekend? Friday? Saturday? Or Thursday, tonight. Except I usually go to bed early on school— Oh, I'm sorry. I didn't mean to say *bed*."

Apparently Gillian can hear every word because she laughs out loud. I cover the phone so Jeremy won't hear her. He's still apologizing.

I have to stop him. "Jeremy, it's okay. I couldn't go out tonight anyway. Too much homework."

"Oh. I see. I understand. I shouldn't have called." He sounds like he's alone in an alley and totally drenched from a cold, pounding rain.

"Jeremy, tomorrow night would be great."

"Nah. That's okay. You don't have to go out with me." I picture Eeyore.

"I'm serious. Come by the dorm tomorrow night."

"Yeah?" I picture ears perking up. "Dinner. And a movie? Or a play? Or museums? But are they open? Or maybe you don't like—"

"Why don't we start with dinner, Jeremy? How about meeting me downstairs at six? Does that work?"

"Six," Jeremy repeats. "Six o'clock?"

No. The year six. "Six o'clock." Then I add, to be safe, "P.M."

We hang up, and I try to convince myself that this is all a good thing. I targeted my un-hot guy, and here we are, headed for a date tomorrow night. I should feel good, victorious, hopeful, eager.

I am none of the above.

The second I hang up, the phone rings again. I exchange grins with Gillian and pick up the receiver. "Jeremy, I told you—"

"Mattie?" The voice doesn't belong to Jeremy Skittles. It's a deep voice, and I recognize it but can't quite place it. "This is Carson Vandermere."

"Carson?" I can't believe he's calling me after the cafeteria disaster.

"So, how's it going?"

"Fine." I rattle my brain, trying to come up with one earthly reason he'd be calling me. *Jake.* "Carson, has something happened to Jake?" My heart is pounding. I picture Jake dangling on the end of a parachute, then falling into the jaws of a shark.

"Jake? He's okay. Anyway, I was wondering if you want to go out this weekend." He exudes confidence. How could he, unless he has amnesia?

"Uh. Sorry, Carson." Lie. "I'm . . . busy this weekend." Half lie.

There's a silence on the other end of the line. I picture Carson the Third sprawled on the floor, having fainted from being turned down for the first time in his life.

"Oops." I tap my desk in a perfect imitation of someone's-at-the-door. Whole lie. "I have to go. Thanks for calling, Carson. See you around."

That night I catch Emma online, and we IM for nearly an hour. I tell her all about my upcoming date with Jeremy Skittles. She fills me in on all the Hamilton news, which takes about two seconds. Then she makes me sign off and hit the books.

After writing 501 words for a 500-word essay and reading two chapters in our history book, I let myself check e-mail again. I have three new e-mails, although two of them want me to lose weight without dieting. I figure it's nothing personal.

The third message is an AOL address, which means it could have come from anybody, anywhere. Gillian and Jake, and probably half the students here, keep their AOL accounts, even though the university lets us use their provider for free. The e-mail could still be an ad. But the header sure looks personal—*Mattie, please read*. Simple. To the point.

How could I not click on it?

```
:: Mattie ::
Please don't think I'm a stalker or anything.
I'm just a guy who'd like to get to know you
better and is afraid that, face-to-face, I
won't say the things I can say in an e-mail. If
I asked you out, and if you actually agreed,
I'd be too worried about what you were thinking
of me. I'd try too hard and would never
communicate the things that might let us get to
know each other. I've been wrestling with this
as I've admired you from a distance (and again,
I promise I'm not a stalker. I won't ask to
meet you in a dark bar or deserted alley.
You're too smart for that anyway). So this is
what I've come up with. And I apologize if it's
too much. If I don't hear from you, I'll keep
writing with no expectations. You can delete me
```

```
with "Lose 15 pounds in one day" ads or the
"Make a million dollars without leaving your
living room" e-mails. It was worth this try.

I realize you may not want to get to know me,
and I'll respect that.

"To give and not expect return, that is what
lies at the heart of love."——Oscar Wilde
```

"Oscar Wilde?"

"Did you say something?" Gillian's at her desk, IMing the love of her life.

I crane my neck around so I can see her. "Gillian, I just got the strangest e-mail."

"Just a minute. Michael's getting off." She types furiously, laughs, types again, then leans back in her chair and sighs. Wheeling the chair to face me, she says, "Okay. What's this about a weird e-mail? Another Bible verse?"

"Nothing like that."

Gillian comes and reads the whole thing over my shoulder. "Hey, girl. Just because somebody claims he's not a stalker, doesn't mean he's not a stalker. Dig?"

I know she's right. But there's something so real about the message. "So you don't think I should answer it?"

"I don't think you should answer it. Why doesn't this Romeo show himself?"

I can't explain it, but I feel the need to defend him. "He said he would eventually. He just wants to get to know me, without the dating thing getting in the way." I reread the e-mail. I *love* Oscar Wilde. That alone makes it impossible for me to delete the message.

But Gillian's right.

"I won't answer it." I log off and get ready for bed.

Gillian tosses three days' worth of clothes off her bed before she climbs in. "Who do you think sent it, Mattie? You have to have some idea."

In the last 10 minutes I've had a hundred ideas. "I can tell you who it's *not* from—Jeremy Skittles."

"Well, that sure narrows the field," Gillian comments. "Anybody been staring at you in your classes? Peeking in our window at night?"

"Gillian!" I climb into my bunk and snuggle under the covers. We've hiked up the AC because both of us like it cold to sleep at night. "I'm thinking it's somebody I haven't really talked with yet." An idea has been forming in the back of my head ever since I read the Oscar Wilde quote. "It could be somebody who appreciates literature. Maybe someone in the English department?" Then it clicks. "The grad assistant! Eric Jensen."

I hang over my bunk so I can see Gillian. "Doesn't that make sense? I haven't seen him, but I'll bet he's seen me. He might even have been around the office. I could have thought he was a prof or a student. People come in and out of there all the time, Gillian."

"Could be," she admits, yawning.

I try to call up some of the unidentified faces I've seen around the English office. For what seems like hours, I rearrange myself in my narrow bed and try to fall asleep.

On Friday, as I walk to the department office, I determine to meet Eric Jensen before the day is over. How hard can it be?

Climbing the steps to the English department, I have to admit that my job isn't quite as exciting as being an English prof. But I still like it. I've run into a couple of the students from when I was Professor Weaver. I've given them each a different explanation, sometimes involving espionage, other times, mental hospitals. So far there have been no serious repercussions.

"Good morning, Mattie," Nancy Colton calls from her desk. She moves the phone so it's exactly perpendicular to the weather radio.

Nancy and I have become pretty good friends. She says I remind her of her daughter, who's now married and living in Phoenix with her husband, the accountant, who plays too much golf, and their three children, April, May, and June. Nancy does not, in any way, remind me of my mother. I don't need a reminder, though. I've written her twice. I even bought a phone card and called her again this morning. A man who didn't sound like Brian answered, so I hung up.

I sit on the corner of Nancy's desk. "Nancy, I need your help. I want to meet the grad assistant."

"Eric?"

"Yeah. Eric. Tell me everything you know about him, Nancy."

She smiles weakly and makes a little circular motion with her finger.

I keep going. "Where is he this hour? How can I—?"

She does the finger motion again. "There's Eric right now." A diplomat, she's not.

I hop off the desk and straighten my skirt, which I've worn for Eric's benefit. Then I turn around, wearing my best smile.

Not bad. Not bad at all.

Eric Jensen is about six feet tall, good build, great hair— brown and thick. He's wearing brown glasses that frame his eyes and make him look intelligent. He's not a Greek god. But nice. Very, very nice. Emma's David verse pops into my head, the one about God not caring so much about the outside. That's the trouble with Em's verses—they always pop up when you least want to hear them.

Eric frowns at me. "Did you want to see me?"

"Eric," Nancy says, before I recover the power of speech, "this is Mattie Mays, our undergraduate assistant."

"The one who rescued me with the video recorder?" He puts air quotes—bending two fingers of each hand toward each other— around "video recorder." I'm never sure why people do this. But he is so cute, I forgive him.

"The very one," I manage to say.

"Thanks." He turns to Nancy. "Could you get Dr. Frost's test folder for me?"

"Mattie can find it for you," Nancy suggests. "She knows the system better than I do."

"Already?" he asks.

I shrug, making a mental note to bring Nancy flowers on Secretaries Day.

"Well, I have to go brew another pot of coffee. If you'll excuse me?" She walks away, leaving us to fend for ourselves.

I will bring flowers *and* candy. I happen to know there's a full pot of coffee in there.

Eric smiles—a very nice smile. "So, Frost's tests?"

I race to the file cabinet and pull out Frost's tests from the F section. Pretty tricky, these files. I walk back with the folder. "How do you like being a grad assistant?" I ask, wishing I had a better line, something that would make him give himself away as my secret e-mailer.

"It's working out pretty well," he answers.

"I'm thinking of majoring in English," I add. The thought has crossed my mind.

"It's a good department. Well, nice to finally meet you, Mattie." His smile is warm, inviting. He sticks out his hand.

I take his hand and shake it. His hands are big and calloused, very manly. I think I'm holding on too long, so I let go.

His hand is still there. "Is that the file?"

Suddenly I realize he's holding out his hand for the file. Not for me. I shove the file at him.

He turns to go again.

I can't stand not knowing if he's the one behind the mystery e-mail. "Eric?" I call after him.

He comes back, frowning.

"Um . . . I just wondered who teaches Oscar Wilde around here." I've read that you should focus on a guy's pupils to tell if he's hiding something. Only I can't remember if the pupils are supposed to get bigger or smaller.

Eric's pupils stay the same. "Oscar Wilde? Christina Wolynski covers Wilde in her 101 class. She's great. You should sign up for her if you like Wilde." There they are again—those air quotes. Maybe it's a sign. "Wild," like a wild date he'd like to have with me? Or it's a clue that he's the one who sent me the "quote"?

"I do—like Wilde, I mean." I have to keep him talking. "And

I met Wolynski. She seems really nice. She was telling me about the football games here. Guess we're supposed to have a great team?"

He breaks into a broad smile—good teeth. He definitely likes me. I think. "We could go all the way this year. It's supposed to be perfect weather for the game tomorrow too."

"Yeah? Guess I'll have to check it out. Hope I can find the field and everything." *Hint, hint.*

I think he's on the verge of gathering courage and asking me to the football game when he hollers over to Nancy, "Mrs. Colton, why don't you give Miss Mays a copy of the university map, the one with Freedom Field on it?" He smiles at me, as if he's fixed everything. "Nice to meet you."

"You too," I manage.

Nancy comes up behind me while I stare at the vanishing figure of Eric Jensen. "I'm only telling you this because you remind me of my own daughter, Mattie. But young men like their young women a little more subtle, dear."

19

"I know it's crazy, Gillian. But I'm really attracted to Eric." I pull on a pair of khaki cargos and a black top. I have no idea how to dress for this date with Jeremy.

"It's not crazy." Gillian brushes lint from my sleeve.

"But I don't think he noticed me. You know, *noticed* me? I'm his Jeremy Skittles."

Gillian laughs. "Girlfriend, you're nobody's Jeremy Skittles. Eric wrote you that mushy stuff in the e-mail, right? So he's probably just shy."

"*Maybe* he wrote it. I don't know that for sure. He knew about Oscar Wilde though. And he did those air quotes a couple of times, like maybe hinting he was the one who sent the quote. Plus, he was the first one to bring up the game tomorrow, how it would be perfect weather and all. I really want him to call and ask me to go with him." I haven't moved two feet from the phone all day, except for class.

"Hey, aren't you late for your Mr. Skittles?"

I have to search my desk for my watch. Gillian's right. It's 10 after 6. "Rats! Poor Jeremy has probably been waiting downstairs for a half hour." I strap on the watch, slip on sandals, and race for the door. "Thanks, Gillian!" I call back. "Guard that phone!"

I tear down the hall and take the stairs to the lobby.

There stands Jeremy Skittles, inches from the elevator. His face lights up when the elevator opens, then fades when it empties. He's wearing a black suit, white shirt, and black tie.

"Hey, Jeremy!" I call, crossing the lobby to him.

He stares at me, not making a move away from the elevator. Kids have to walk around him. His mouth opens. Finally, words come out. "You came?"

*

Jeremy Skittles

Mattie Mays is even prettier than I remembered from class. But she's wearing tan jeans with pockets on the sides. If I were a football player, I'll bet she would have worn a dress. That's the way it always is. "I made a reservation at Henri's." I clear my throat. "It's French."

"*Magnifique!*" She heads for the door.

I have to hurry to keep up with her. She might be making a run for it. I trip over a crack in the sidewalk and hope she didn't notice.

"Watch your step there, Jeremy."

She noticed.

I point to Mother's silver Park Avenue. I had to drive around the lot for 20 minutes until someone backed out of the front row. And I still had to wait a half hour on her. But she's so pretty. I wish Robbie and Martin could see me now. I know there's no way she's smart enough for me, even though her answers in history class sound intelligent. She probably doesn't know anything about quantum physics or molecular biology.

I open the door for her, and she slides in.

"Nice wheels, Jeremy," she says.

"It's okay." No need to tell her the car isn't mine.

I get in and start the engine. I'm so nervous that I turn the key again and get that grinding noise Mother hates.

"So, Jeremy, do you have any brothers or sisters?"

"No." Why would she want to know that? It's none of her business.

"I don't either. It's tough being an only child, don't you think?"

I shrug. I've always been glad I don't have siblings.

"Do your parents live in California?"

I wish she'd stop talking. Backing out of the parking space takes all my concentration.

"My mother lives here," I answer. I'm not the only college guy living at home, and it's none of her business anyway.

I don't really like to drive because accidents are everywhere, waiting to happen to somebody. So I keep well under the speed limit when we get on the freeway. Our dinner reservation isn't until eight. I didn't want to be late.

"Speed limit's 55 here, Jeremy," Mattie informs me.

"Speed kills," I tell her. It's one of my mother's favorite sayings.

"And slow infuriates," she mumbles.

I act like I don't hear. I might have known that somebody this pretty would travel in the fast lane. I know girls like that, although I've never gone out with any of them.

She makes small talk, but I'm trying to get to the right lane because our exit is coming up before long.

"Do you mind?" She turns on the radio. Then, without even asking, she changes the station to jazz. "Don't you love Coltrane?"

I've never heard of Coltrane, but I fake it. "Yes." I leave it on as long as I can stand it, which is until I have to leave the freeway. Then I turn it off.

I pull slowly into the parking lot of Henri's and see a couple of spaces not too far from the front. It's the first time I've driven here myself, and I had no idea how tiny the parking spaces are. It takes me three tries to get into one of them.

Mattie's staring out of the window as I turn off the engine, and I'm afraid I'm blowing it already. She thinks I'm not cool enough for her. I reach across her and get Mother's pack of Camels from the glove compartment. "Want a smoke before we go in?"

"I don't smoke," she answers.

I can't believe it. Now I don't know whether to try to smoke or to make some excuse because I don't smoke either.

"Do you really have to smoke, Jeremy?" she asks. "I have a real problem with secondhand smoke. Maybe you could do it outside?"

Relieved, I shrug and return the pack to the glove compartment.

By the time I make it to her car door, she has it open and is getting out.

"Parking lot looks really full," she observes. "They must be busy."

"It's okay. I made a reservation."

"Good thinking, Jeremy. I'm starving."

About a dozen people are waiting in the overflow outside, with more couples lining up inside.

Mattie clears her throat. "Do you want to check on our reservation?"

"Sure. Yeah." I make my way to the front of the line, where a woman with a clipboard stands at a podium. I clear my throat. She doesn't look up. I clear it louder. Still no eye contact.

"Excuse me?" It's Mattie. "Do you have a reservation for Jeremy Skittles?"

The woman smiles at Mattie. "Let me see." She runs her finger down the clipboard, then shakes her head. "Skittles? Nope. I don't see it."

"Look again!" I demand. This can't be happening. Mother said she phoned the restaurant. She never makes a mistake like this.

The woman shakes her head again. "I'm sorry. When was the reservation?"

"Eight o'clock," I answer.

"Eight?" Mattie repeats.

The woman chuckles. "Ah. Okay." She turns the page and runs her finger down another list. "Yes. Here you are." She looks up. "You have quite a wait. Want me to put you on the current waiting list? I think that might come up sooner." She hands me the wooden block, rimmed with tiny red lights.

"This lights up and vibrates when it's our turn," I inform Mattie, attempting to regain control.

"Cool. Let's wait outside though. It's pretty stuffy in here."

We thread through the crowd to the brick front of Henri's.

"How are you liking your classes so far, Jeremy?" She leans against the white brick wall.

"I was hoping they would be more challenging." Actually, university work has turned out to be harder than I'd anticipated.

"I really like our history class," Mattie continues. "Don't you? When Professor Brown was talking about the no-fly zone—wasn't that interesting?"

I can't believe my luck. Last night I watched a special on Fox News, a roundtable discussion on the no-fly zone in the Middle East. "Let me tell you what's wrong with Dr. Brown's interpretation of that policy," I begin. I can remember every argument, so I repeat them all for her. It takes at least 10 minutes, and Mattie listens the whole time, without interrupting. When I sum it all up, I ask her if she has any questions.

She narrows her eyes. "Do you think it's a good idea to call in a SWAT team to a no-fly zone?" Then she grins.

"I don't think that's necessary."

We're quiet so long that I'm getting nervous. A guy walks up the sidewalk, and I recognize him. "Isn't that guy in our history class?" His date has reddish hair and a dress that's too low-cut for my taste.

Mattie looks, then waves. "Jake! Where did you—?" She stops, and her smile fades. "Val?"

The girl loops her arm through Jake's. Jake looks like he's been caught with his hand in the cookie jar.

The girl waves. "Matilda Mays! Imagine running into you. Feels like old times." She puts her head on Jake's shoulder.

Jake walks up. "Jeremy, right? Valerie, this is Jeremy. Jeremy, Valerie."

Mattie squints into Valerie's face. "Val, you have something on your cheek."

I don't see anything, but Valerie rubs her cheek furiously. "Did I get it?"

Mattie keeps staring and shakes her head. "No. Right there." She touches her own cheekbone.

Valerie rubs harder. "Did I get it?"

Jake glares at Mattie, then tells his date, "You got it. Trust me. There's nothing there."

Valerie looks relieved. "Good. I need to go to the ladies' room and freshen my makeup."

"Good idea," Mattie agrees.

"Third door on your left," I inform her.

Valerie struts off.

"Well, fancy meeting you here, huh?" Jake says.

"Fancy meeting you—and *Val*—here," Mattie snaps. "Didn't you learn anything in high school?"

"We kind of ran into each other."

"What happened to her football player?"

Jake shrugs. "I guess she dumped him."

"*He* dumped *her*, more likely."

I get the feeling I'm missing something.

Jake sighs. "My reservation's for 7:00. Better get going. You guys should have called ahead."

"I called ahead," I correct him.

Mattie and I wait forever until the wooden square explodes in my hands. I drop it. The red lights flash.

Mattie picks it up. "Yea! We win!" She jumps in the air like a cheerleader. "Hurray for us!"

All around us people laugh. The couple behind us applauds. I feel my face heat with embarrassment.

Mattie grabs my arm and pulls me to the front of the line. The hostess has abandoned her post.

"Excuse me!" barks a short white-haired woman behind me. "We're waiting here."

"Sorry." Mattie waves the buzzer. "Our buzzer went off."

"So did ours. About 10 minutes ago."

"Ours too!" A man holds up his flashing wooden square. So do four other couples.

"That hostess is slow as molasses," the old woman complains as the hostess returns.

"I apologize." The hostess grabs a stack of menus. "We're supposed to have two working this shift. Sharon called in sick."

To my horror, Mattie moves around behind the podium and exchanges whispers with the hostess. The hostess leaves with the older couple. Then Mattie turns to the crowd. *"Trés bien! Alors . . ."* She consults the list in front of her. "This way, please— the Pentos and Baumans?" If I didn't know better, I'd swear she was French.

Two couples march up to the podium.

"Voilá! S'il vous plait," Mattie says. "The-e-ez way."

I stand off to the side, mortified, as my date acts as a French hostess, ushering customers to tables one by one, bringing them menus and glasses of water. The real hostess lets her do it too, and even thanks her.

Finally Mattie takes my arm and gets us our own table. I pull out her chair to seat her.

She slides in. "Cool. You're a scholar and a gentleman."

I'm not sure if she's making fun of me or not. But she's smiling. I have a feeling she doesn't date many polite men.

"That's a really nice suit, Jeremy." She picks up the menu and studies it, then peers over the top. "Men are lucky that way. Did you ever think about how men get to wear basically one outfit to everything their whole lives? To church, on a date, to a business meeting, to teach, to get married . . . to their own funeral."

"No." I haven't thought about it, and I don't know anyone else who would have. She's making me nervous, like there might be something wrong with her.

Mattie is still studying the menu when the waitress finally arrives.

I haven't had to consult the menu. I know every item they serve here. "We'll have two filet mignons." I use my best French accent, which earned me straight As in high school. "Potatoes au gratin, *et haricots verts*." I can't remember the word for iced tea. "Um . . . we'll have iced tea and a salad too." I glance at Mattie to see if she's impressed.

She closes her menu. "Guess I didn't need this, huh?"

"How would you like your steak?" the waitress asks.

"Rare." Mother says it's the only way the taste comes through.

"Extra well done, please. No pink at all. Thanks." Mattie hands over our menus, and the waitress turns to go.

"It's really much better with the juices," I tell her, taking a slice of sesame bread from the basket.

"No doubt."

We talk about my honors classes while Mattie eats four slices of the bread. Then the waitress brings our salads.

"My high school physics teacher knew more about physics than Professor Laird," I tell her.

"Uh-huh." She keeps checking over her shoulder, back where Jake and the redhead are sitting.

About halfway through our entrée, I run out of classes to discuss. Mattie eats less than half her steak and asks for a doggie bag. "It was really good, Jeremy. Thanks. Are you going to eat the rest of the bread?"

When I shake my head no, she wraps up the rest of the loaf and puts it in her doggie bag.

I give the waitress Mother's credit card. Then we walk outside. The wind has kicked up, and I have to keep one hand on my tie and the other on my hair.

"Jeremy, look! See?" She's pointing to the sky.

I don't see anything but a flock of birds. You'd think she'd spotted a movie star.

"Those birds!" she exclaims. "Did you see them take off? There! See them change directions, all at once? Don't you *love* that? I feel it in here. I don't know why." She puts her hand over her heart, as if she's going to recite the Pledge of Allegiance.

"They're probably just crows or grackle," I explain.

I have to jog to the car to open the door before Mattie does.

She thanks me, and I walk around to my side, conscious that she's probably watching me as I pass in front of the car. I hope my hair hasn't gotten messed up.

I climb in, put on my seat belt, and turn the key. Nothing happens.

I try it again. Sweat beads on my forehead. I try again. The engine makes a noise like a toy car, then stops. I can't believe this is happening to me.

"Don't tell me you've run out of gas on a lonely road," Mattie says.

"No! The needle is on *F*. I filled up this afternoon."

"I'm kidding, Jere. Try it again."

I try it again. This time there's a noise, then a click. Then nothing.

Mattie gets out of the car. "Pop the hood!" she demands.

I look for something that will open the hood. I feel along the dash and the steering wheel.

Mattie opens my door and reaches down by my foot. Something clicks, and the hood moves. "It's tricky," she says. "The latch is hard to find on Buicks." She closes my door and goes to the front of the car. Then she opens the hood and sticks her head in.

I survey the parking lot. A few people are watching us. I want to slide down the seat and out of sight.

"Now try it!" Mattie calls.

Of course, it doesn't work.

Mattie comes to the driver's side. "Do you have jumper cables?"

I have no idea. "I—I don't—"

"No sweat. I'll go get Jake."

Mattie runs inside and in a minute returns with Jake, who jogs to the end of the parking lot, while Mattie does who-knows-what under the hood of the Park Avenue. I hear a rattle and a noise I'd expect to hear on a drag strip or racetrack. Then an old, rusted, banged-up car sputters up to *my mother's* car, almost touching hood to hood.

"Mattie, be careful!" I holler out of the window.

"Relax, Jeremy!" she yells back, waving Jake to pull the hideous car even closer to Mother's.

Relax is the last thing I could do. I strain to see Jake hand Mattie cables that she attaches under the Buick's hood, while he fastens them under the rattletrap's hood.

"Start her up!" Mattie commands.

I do as I'm told, and the engine catches. Mattie unhooks the cables and tosses them to Jake. They exchange words I can't make out. I think she's thanking him. But then they both wave their arms, and their voices get louder, although I can't make out what they're saying.

Jake storms off, and Mattie yells something after him, but he doesn't turn around. He is the only one in the parking lot who doesn't.

She gets in and buckles her seat belt. "You need to get your electrical checked out."

I think about asking her how she knows so much about cars, but I don't think I want to know.

We exit the freeway, and I start to change lanes when Mattie cries, "No! Pull off to the side, Jeremy."

"What?" I slow down, but it's a bad part of the neighborhood. Instinctively I check to make sure the doors are locked. "Your dorm is this way."

"Yeah. Pull over for a second." She's unbuckling her seat belt.

I pull over. Before I can stop her, she springs from the car with her doggie bag and runs straight to a tramp. Now I *know* there's something wrong with her.

After a minute she hops back in. "Thanks, Jeremy. I thought my friend could use the food. He's had a horrible year. Anyway, thanks for stopping."

I don't ask. Mattie has her flaws, her faults. But I can't let that get in the way of our relationship. In time she will change. People change when they move to California.

I escort her to her dorm. Couples are hugging and kissing outside as we walk up the sidewalk. Mattie keeps looking up at the sky, and I think she's probably nervous, wondering if I'll kiss her good night. Even thinking this makes me break out in a sweat. I'll keep her guessing, keep her off balance. Then I'll kiss her good night on our next date.

This date hasn't gone as smoothly as I would have liked. I take a look at her while her head is tilted toward the sky. She is so pretty. And I didn't run into anyone I know, except Jake. Robbie and Martin won't even believe me when I tell them I had a date with her. Maybe next time I'll arrange for them to be at the same place so they can see for themselves.

"Well, thanks for dinner, Jeremy." She sticks out her hand. I see grease on her fingers.

I manage to shake her hand without touching her fingers, but it isn't easy. Her handshake is firm. "So, where do you want to go next time?" I ask. "Do you want to go out tomorrow night?" I'm thinking I should strike while the iron's hot. She's just been to a nicer restaurant than she's probably ever eaten in. And she's been riding in a very nice car.

"I've got too much work to do this weekend," she answers. "But thanks anyway."

"So next week? Friday? or Saturday?"

"Maybe you better call me, Jeremy. Okay?"

"Call me" is good. Definitely good. "I'll call you." I have to start taking the lead in this relationship. "We'll go to a movie."

She smiles. "Well, thanks again. Night, Jeremy. And don't forget to take care of that electrical problem."

I stroll back to the car. I can hardly wait to go out with Mattie Mays again.

Mattie

I trudge up the steps to my dorm room, thinking that this has been the longest night in the history of womankind. I would give up to half of my kingdom—so that would be a pair of jeans and about 12 books—for a good night's sleep.

Gillian's gone home for the weekend, and I thought I'd be happy to have the room to myself. But opening the door to the empty room, which is exactly like I left it—no music, no clothes on my bed—gives me a pang of loneliness. I picture Gillian at home with her parents and little brothers and wonder what it would feel like to go home to a family like that.

The phone rings, and I pick it up automatically. "Hello?"

"Hello, Mattie. This is Jeremy Skittles. I wondered if you'd thought about it. Would you like to go out on a date with me on Saturday? Not this Saturday, because you have homework. But next Saturday?"

"I don't think so, Jeremy." I can't believe he's calling me so soon. I should have Naomi give him the phone rules.

"That's okay. I'll call back when you're not so tired." He hangs up before I can tell him not to bother calling back.

As tired as I am, I know I won't sleep until I can talk to Em. She's not online, so I write her an e-mail.

:: Dear Em ::
Sometimes you <u>can</u> judge a book by its cover, and the inside turns out to be a lot like the outside. So much for my "un-hot" date. Jeremy is probably a very nice person. But Em, he doesn't get it! A flock of birds took off almost in front of us, and he didn't feel it. You know how I love that—the way you feel those wings inside you. I spotted the Little Dipper for the first time in the L.A. sky tonight, and I couldn't share it with my date.

Plus, he ordered for me! I honestly think he believes I'm an idiot. But I shouldn't take it personally. He believes all girls are idiots—in fact, all people not named Jeremy Skittles.

I didn't mind that he was driving his mother's car (at glacier speed) and wanted me to believe it was his. But they both smoke. I'll have to wash everything three times to get rid of the stench.

A night with Jeremy Skittles should have been punishment enough, right? But who should we run into but your brother and—brace yourself, Em— VAL! She was all over him too. Jake claims Val's football boyfriend broke her heart, and he's only consoling the poor girl. Right. Here he goes again. Jake and I kind of got into it

```
in  the  parking  lot.  I  guess  I  said  some  things
I  shouldn't.  But  honestly,  Em.  Val  Ramsey?

Don't  you  worry,  though.  I  can  handle  Val.  And
you  can  leave  your  brother  to  me.  If  I  can't
find  Mr.  Right,  the  least  I  can  do  is  save  Jake
from  Ms.  Wrong.
```

The *New Mail* box pops up on my screen with a *ding* that makes me jump and feel like an idiot for it. Maybe Em and I are writing at the same time.

I click on the message but see it's from my mystery e-mailer. I'm a lot more excited than I should be.

I click back to Emma's e-mail.

```
Em,  remember  I  told  you  about  that  e-mail  I  got
from  some  guy  who  says  he  wants  to  get  to  know
me?  You  said  I  should  ignore  it,  and  I  have.
But  it's  getting  harder.  I  just  got  another
message  from  my  secret  admirer.  I'll  send  this
now  and  then  let  you  know  what  the  new  message
says.

Love,  Midnight  Mattie
```

I hurry back to the mystery e-mail.

```
Hi,  again.  I  apologize  (again)  if  this  is
freaking  you  out  in  any  way.  Seriously,  say  the
word  and  I  won't  send  any  more  e-mails.  I  know
the  kinds  of  things  going  on  in  cyberspace
these  days.  I  don't  want  you  to  be  worried  for
a  minute.  You  have  no  reason  to  believe  me  when
I  tell  you  that  you  know  me  a  little  bit  and
aren't  scared  of  me  in  person.  It  must  seem
crazy  anyway  that  a  guy  would  want  to  get  to
```

know you, your words, and let you get to know
him, before dating. I can't blame you if you
don't understand.

So I *do* know my mystery e-mailer! I picture Eric. Maybe after he left me in the English department, the poor guy beat himself up for not being able to talk more openly with me. Maybe he worried about it all night and is only now getting gutsy enough to write.

The e-mail goes on, talking about friendship being better than dating, sharing what's really important, rather than trying to look good. It makes me think about endless conversations Emma, Jake, and I have had on moon check nights, lying on the hood of Jake's car. I can't help feeling drawn to Eric as he writes this. The message ends—

I don't think most people who know me would
believe me if I told them I'm fearful. But I
know I am. I'm afraid of needing or depending
on anyone. I'm afraid of trembling when I
finally get the courage to tell you who's
writing these crazy messages. But I'm also
afraid of being alone.

I better stop before you think I'm a total
loser. Thanks for reading.

Maybe it's because it's so late. Or maybe there's some other reason. But I can't stop myself. I hit *Reply*.

Soteriophobia——that's fear of dependence on
others. And tremophobia's the fear of
trembling. The fear of ending up or being
alone that's isolophobia. I know because I have
them too.

Nite.

———Mattie

I lie in bed, waiting for sleep for an hour. I try not to think, but I can't get Eric out of my head—his boyish, handsome face, the way his big brown eyes shift away when I look at him. Finally I can't take it anymore. I climb out of the bunk and click on the desk lamp. A golden streak of light spreads over my desk, and I turn on the computer and log on.

I reread the mystery e-mail and hit *Reply*. Then I type as fast as I can,

```
I have another fear—going to the football game
by myself. I'll be here all morning.
```

———Mattie

Before I can change my mind, I hit *Send*.

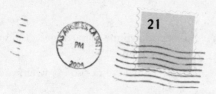

21

Saturday morning I wake up early. For a second I can't remember if I actually wrote Eric back, or if I dreamed it. Did I really tell him I'm afraid to go to the game alone? I might as well wear a sign, like Albert's—*Will work for a date to the football game.* Naomi would kill me if she knew.

Part of me wants to crawl under a rock, but the other part of me is starting to come alive with hope, hope that Eric will get the confidence he needs from this e-mail and call me. So I wait by the phone.

I'm zipping up my best jeans when the phone rings. Yes! I lunge for the receiver and ram my toe into the chair. "Ow!" I grab the phone and try to sound casual, in spite of hopping on one foot and holding my throbbing toe. "Hello?" I sound too anxious. First I beg Eric to phone me, and now I sound like I'm waiting for his call. Never mind that I am.

"Hello, Mattie."

The voice is wrong. All wrong.

"Hello? Mattie? Are you there? This is Jeremy. Jeremy Skittles?"

I sink to the floor, suddenly feeling like my bones have dissolved. "Hello, Jeremy." I stare at Gillian's alarm clock. "Jeremy, it's 7:52 on a Saturday morning."

"Oh. Did I wake you?" He doesn't wait for my answer. "I wanted to let you know what time I'll pick you up tonight."

"What?"

He clears his throat. I think he's trying macho on for size. It doesn't fit. "Seven. That's it. I'll pick you up at—"

"Jeremy, we don't have a date."

"Then I'll pick you up—"

"No, Jeremy." I have to beat down my rising anger. "I'm sorry if I led you on. We had a nice dinner, but—"

"That's okay. I'll call you when you're not so . . . when you've had a chance to wake up. Good-bye."

I stare at the silent receiver until the disconnected phone buzz kicks in. Then I hang up fast. Eric might be trying to call. He may have tried already and gotten a busy signal.

All morning I wait for the phone to ring. I bargain with it. "Please, please ring. I'll never yell into you again. I'll hang up gently." It makes no sound. I reason with it. "Look, just one ring. I'll pick it up before the second ring. All you have to do is carry Eric's voice through your little wires. . . ."

I threaten. "Ring! Now! Right now—or I'm throwing you out the window! I'll twist your cord so tight you won't be able to breathe!"

Nothing.

Kickoff is at noon. That's when I give up. I turn on the radio and hear the crowd noise in the background. I am missing the first game of my college career. I'm no chick when it comes to football. Thanks to Jake, Emma and I knew more about the game than most of Jake's high school buddies.

I listen to the entire first half on the radio while lying on my back in bed, feeling sorrier and sorrier for myself. When the Squirrels head for the lockers, it's a 7-7 tie. I want to tell the quarterback he should use Maxwell, the fullback, more . . . and try a draw play, first possession. I miss analyzing the game with Jake and Emma at halftime, the way we did in high school.

I roll over and gaze out at the sunshine. It's a gorgeous after-noon, and here I am, lying in bed, complaining. "Mattie Mays," I say aloud, "get a move on."

I jog to the football field and get there just as the Flying Squirrels are kicking off for the second half. Crowd noise soars as if I've turned up the radio. My student ID gets me through the gate, and I find a decent spot in the bleachers. I am surrounded by cou-ples—Delta Gammas and their dates in front of me, and some frat guys and their dates behind me. I get stares, but nobody orders me to leave their section. And I try not to feel like the only person here without a date.

When the hot dog vendor yells down our aisle, I wave at him and decide I'm going to enjoy myself. "Two hot dogs!" I holler.

He sets down the silver mini-oven he wears around his waist and loads up two dogs for me. I pass a $20 bill down the long row. My dogs and every cent of my change pass through 20-plus hands and land safely in my own outstretched hand. That's my favorite part about games—the fact that you can trust perfect strangers, probably thieves and axe murderers, with your money at a ball game. That's America.

Nothing happens until the Squirrels' second possession. Then the quarterback goes to Maxwell, who runs the ball down the 60, 50, 40, 30, 20, 10 yard line. "Touchdown!" I scream.

We're all on our feet, congratulating each other, like we're old friends, like we've run that ball the length of the field ourselves.

It's all our game the rest of the way, and we bring in our first victory 28-10.

Coming back to the dorm, I have to weave through scores of hand-holding couples and several guy groups that smell like a brew-ery. To escape the crowd I duck down a side street and take the long way around, detouring under the freeway to look for Albert. He's not there, but I meet two friends of his. I forgot to carry granola bars, so I give them the hot dog change and ask them to tell Albert hi for me.

Winding back through the rec area behind Jake's dorm, I'm pretty sure I see Jake dribbling in a half-court game.

I stroll down to the court just as Jake shoots and misses. "Nice shot, Jake. You dropped your elbow."

"Mattie!" Carson Vandermere cries, grabbing Jake's rebound. He fires it to a tall, thin guy, who would make Wilt the Stilt look short. The guy stuffs it. Carson jogs over to me. "How's everything going?"

"Hey, Carson. Good. How about you?"

"Matt!" Jake hollers. "Come play. I'm getting killed."

"*You're* getting killed? Pretty embarrassing, Jake."

"Carson!" Jake shouts. "Matt and I will take you and Syd two-on-two."

"I don't know, man," says the tree-tall guy, who just stuffed the basket practically flat-footed.

"Do you play?" Carson looks pretty skeptical.

I grin at Jake.

"She plays." Jake grins back. "Game to 11?"

We let Carson and Syd—that's the giant's name—have the ball first. Syd shoots over my block and scores.

"Okay." Jake takes the ball out. "Don't say we didn't give you a chance."

I move to my appointed spot. Jake taught Emma and me to play basketball when we were barely old enough to hold the ball. For years he could beat us one-on-two, without breaking a sweat. Then I discovered that I have a no-miss zone. It's to the right and behind the free-throw arch, in the three-point range. I started hitting shots from there when I was 10. Then I practiced and practiced from that spot, until I almost never miss. I can't do layups anymore. I'm not that great at free throws. But give me the ball in *my* spot, and I'll sink it easily nine out of 10 times, or better.

Jake gives me the ball in the inbound pass. I aim and shoot. Nothing but net.

"That's three!" Jake announces.

"Sweet!" Carson exclaims. "How'd you do that?"

I shrug. "Pure luck."

Jake steals the ball from Carson. I haven't moved from my spot, since the chances of me blocking Syd's shot are about as good as Jeremy's odds of winning the Indy 500. Jake bounces the ball to me. I shoot and score.

"Six-two!" Jake cries.

Carson scores on an inbound pass. I get away with another unguarded shot, making it nine to four. Then Syd smothers me and won't let me shoot from my spot. He intercepts my pass and puts it in. Nine to seven.

I hold the ball out of bounds, and Jake signs to me, *Throw it to me fast. Bounce it between Syd's legs. Then get to your spot.*

"Hey, what are you doing?" Syd asks Jake.

"Nothing illegal," he answers.

That's what Em used to say about our basketball sign language—*All of it legal, none of it fair.*

I manage to bounce the ball between Syd's long legs. Jake scrambles and gets it, but Carson won't let him move to the basket. I act like I'm closing in. Syd follows me. Then I race back to my spot. Jake fires me the ball. I shoot, and that's the ball game.

"We should have bet on the game, Matt." Jake gives me a high five.

"You know Emma made us promise not to take sucker bets."

"Good game." Syd bends way down to shake my hand. He has a nice smile. "We ought to recruit you for the Squirrels."

"Syd plays varsity ball too," Jake informs me.

Carson hasn't stopped staring at me. I check my shirt to make sure I haven't sweat through. "Mattie," he says, scratching his head, "you're really something. Where did you learn to play ball like that?"

Jake grins, as if he's the proud father.

"Where did I learn to play? From Jake's sister." I enjoy wiping the smirk off Jake's face.

Carson and Jake walk me back to the dorm. We pass the Flying Squirrel and take turns rubbing the nose.

"Did you see the football game?" Carson asks.

"Great game." I turn to Jake. "Did you see that freshman, Baxter, the defensive back they put in at the end of the fourth quarter? I like him a lot. He'll be good. I hope they give him more play-ing time."

"I was thinking the same thing," Jake fires back. "Did you catch his fake on third down—"

"Twenty-three yard line? That was so tight."

Carson flashes me his million-dollar smile. "Mattie, don't tell me you play football like you play basketball."

"Armchair quarterback only."

We cut through the parking lot behind my dorm. I happen to gaze over a row of cars, and who should I see locked tighter than handcuffs and leaning against a yellow convertible? Dear ol' Val . . . and her supposedly ex-boyfriend football player.

"Hi, Val!" I call as loud as I can. Jake shouldn't miss this.

Valerie frowns and looks around until she sees me waving at her.

"How's it going?" I yell.

Jake's staring at her too now. "Stop it, Matt."

For a second I feel bad. I don't want to hurt Jake. But I don't want Val to get away with lying to him. She and her football guy haven't broken up. She was probably using Jake to make the guy jealous. "I'm sorry, Jake," I whisper.

He shrugs. "No big deal."

"So, you guys want to do anything?" Carson asks.

I shake my head. "Too much homework. Thanks anyway. Take it easy—both of you."

I work pretty hard for a couple hours until Jake calls and wants to go postcard shopping.

"Come on, Matt. I can't pick out postcards myself. We'll be fast. You can use the break. If we stock up now, we won't have to do this every week."

Jake comes by, and we walk two blocks to Cards 'n' More. I head for the card racks and hope postcards count as cards.

"Matt! Check this out!" Jake's voice comes from the next aisle. Then a pumpkin candle sails over the top of the aisle divider.

I race down the aisle and catch the orange candle before it lands on a shelf of glass elves. "Grow up, Jake!" I scold. I'm carefully setting the candle on the elf shelf when something red flies over the card rack. Reflexes kick in, and I grab it in midair. It's a glass Christmas ornament.

"Jake!"

He pokes his head around. "It deserves to be broken, Matt. You can't start selling Christmas things before Halloween."

You'd think that I'd know better than to go shopping with Jake Jackson. I have to get him away from the breakables. Besides, the "more" in Cards 'n' More does not include postcards.

"Let's get out of here," Jake urges. "Race you to the parking lot!"

I try to catch him, but he's too fast. He has the doors unlocked by the time I get there. At least I beat him getting into the car. It starts on the first try but sounds like the accelerator is stuck. "I don't like the idle," I tell him. "Back it out. See if it settles. We ought to change to lighter weight oil out here."

He backs out, and the motor cuts down.

I don't want to forget to check the engine later, so I call up my memory hook. Emma, Jake, and I learned the memory system from an old book I got at a library sale. We memorized 10 hooks, or memory triggers. One is alarm clock. Two is jeans. Three is chair. Four is table. And so on. We can remember any list of 10 items by linking each item to one of the memory hooks and forming a mental picture. The wilder the image, the better you remember. Sounds crazy, but it works.

"We have to remember to check your engine, Jake. Picture your alarm going off in the morning and your car exploding into a million pieces."

Jake frowns. "Nice thought, Matt. Thanks." He hasn't fastened his seat belt.

"Jake, put on your seat belt. What's the matter with you?"

"Nothing's the matter with me."

"Right. Nothing that a little brain transplant wouldn't fix." I'm remembering what Carson said about Jake's daredevil parasailing.

Lips pursed, Jake fastens his seat belt. "You know, Mattie, you could at least try to be nicer."

"I'll try to be nicer, if you'll try to be smarter." I think I'm extra mad because I keep imagining Jake's alarm going off and the car exploding. And somehow Jake's in the picture without a seat belt.

Jake heads out of campus, but he's not speaking to me.

"Want to swing by and see how Albert's doing?" I suggest.

Jake swerves and takes a different route.

"That's mature, Jake." He may be Em's older brother, but he's always been the baby.

He still isn't speaking to me.

"Okay. I'm sorry I yelled at you, Jake." I bite my tongue because I want so much to add the "but"—as in, "but you're a stupidhead for not wearing your seat belt and for needing to take risks all the time." *Stupidhead* is a word Emma and I invented, mainly for Jake, when we were little kids. It still works.

"Yeah. Me too."

"Besides," I add, "I can only please one person a day. And it's simply not your day. Tomorrow's not looking good either. Sorry."

He grins. He can't help it. The dimple on his cheek burrows deeper. Then it disappears, along with the smile. "You're right about it not being my day, though. I saw Stella at the game with some yahoo."

"He won't stand a chance once she gets to know you, Jake." Emma is much better with these pep talks than I'll ever be. "Don't forget. You've got logic class together. Sooner or later, she'll give in to your charm, right?"

"Charm? That prof will have me looking like an idiot in every class, Matt. I never should have taken it."

I don't think I've ever seen Jake like this. "Is he really that bad? Isn't he like that with everybody?"

"That's just the thing, Matt. If he picked on everybody, made everybody look stupid, I could live with that. But he doesn't. I think he knows how I feel about Stella."

Anger wads up inside me. Profs have too much power. Somebody ought to knock this one down a few notches.

"Matt?" Jake is eyeing me suspiciously. "You've got that look in your eye."

"Hmmm?" What I'm thinking is that it may be time for me to drop in on Professor Nettles' logic class. But Jake will be better off if he doesn't know this.

I change the subject. "So, where are we going?" I haven't been paying much attention, but we're on a highway I don't recognize. I roll down the window, and the air has changed. It feels different and smells . . . salty? "Jake, are we close to the ocean?"

"We're always close to the ocean. I thought we might have better luck with postcards down by the beach."

I have never seen an ocean, not live and in person. I guess I knew I would see one here, eventually. But I'm as excited as if it were Christmas. Then I spot it. Between buildings, at the end of a street, a patch of blue spreads like a reflection of the sky. "Jake, that's the ocean!"

He smiles at me. "Nothing gets by you, does it, Matt?"

"I smell salt, and fish, and . . . something else . . . sun! I can smell the sun, Jake." I know I'm grinning like a crazy person, but I can't stop. "I wish Em were here."

"Me too."

Jake starts to drive into a lot where you have to pay seven dollars, no matter how long you stay there. But I make him circle the streets until we find a free parking space. "I probably burned up seven bucks in gas, Matt," he grumbles.

We get out of the car, and I take deep breaths until my head feels light. I think I hear waves splashing the shore, even though we're yards from the beach. But the waves are drowned out by little kids screaming. A dozen kinds of music battle for airwaves. Skates and blades whir on pavement. Someone's singing off-key.

"Saturday at the beach," Jake observes.

We thread through parked cars to a broad sidewalk, lined with small shops and booths, selling everything from pipes to guitars to every T-shirt you could imagine. Farther down, vendors have jewelry, velvet pictures, statues, and trinkets spread out on blankets. Beyond that, people are drawing or singing or making paper flowers in exchange for donations tossed into upside-down hats.

"Jake, we need granola bars."

"I know." He sighs. "Could we get postcards first?"

"First . . ." I hold onto Jake's arm to steady myself while I unbuckle my sandals. "I have a date with the Pacific. Jake, I can't get this close to the ocean and not go in."

"We don't have suits, Matt."

"I'm just going to wade." I take off through the white sand. It's hot, but my soles are so calloused from walking barefoot that it doesn't hurt. "Come on, Jake!" I holler back.

Close to the water, the sand hardens, like clay. Waves lap in big arcs. A skinny kid on a bright yellow mini-surfboard runs and jumps on the board, catching the wave on the sand and skimming across the shore.

I gaze out at the ocean and stand perfectly still. Only it feels like I'm on a boat in the waves.

"You okay, Matt?" Jake comes up behind me.

"Jake, I'm dizzy." The ground moves when I close my eyes.

Jake laughs. "It does that to you, especially your first time at the ocean." He puts his hand on my shoulder to steady me. "You'll be all right in a minute."

It's longer than a minute, but I don't mind a bit. I gaze at the sky, then the ocean. And I'm moving with them. Something rises inside me, and I'm surprised to discover it's prayer, or praise, or something very like that. *God, you made all this. What a great job! Thank you for letting me be here and see it and feel it.* It may be the most natural, spontaneous prayer I've ever prayed, and I can't wait to tell Emma.

"God did good, didn't he, Jake?"

"That sounds like something Emma would say."

I smile up at him. "Thanks."

Pretty soon the world stops tilting. I run into the waves, as deep as I can without embarrassing myself. The cold water jolts my system and makes me laugh out loud.

A Spanish-speaking family of six is building a castle a few feet up from us. They're staring at me, and the two boys are laughing.

"It's my first time in the ocean!" I shout.

The father nods, and the little girl smiles at me.

"No kidding," observes a young guy who paddles his Styrofoam board past me, splashing me as he kicks.

A wave comes, and the guy topples off the board and disappears underwater. His board floats. I grab it and walk it over to him when he surfaces. He thanks me and climbs up again, as if the board is a bronco.

Jake would let me stay and play as long as I want, but I know he's got things to do. I look around for him and don't see him. I scan the water. He's not there either. For a second I can't breathe. Then I spot him, sitting on a rock, and *I* feel like a stupidhead for being panicked.

I join him, not mentioning the panic attack.

He holds up a brown bag. "Gatorade and granola bars. Now, can we get those postcards?"

We drop our food into the upside-down hats as we walk to the end of the row of shops.

The last three stores have spinning wire racks of postcards out front. At store #1, we take two seconds to reject all the cards, which even make Jake blush. In the next shop, we split up. I grab several postcards of the ocean because Em has to see it. But none of them will make her *feel* it.

"So, what did you come up with?" Jake asks, peering over my shoulder at the display of postcards. He takes my stack out of my hand. "Nine of the ocean? Matt, come on. I thought we were supposed to get cards that go with our Love Rules. They can't all be about the ocean."

"Guess I got a little carried away," I admit. "What did you come up with?"

He shows me his stack. They're all pretty weird, but it's hard to know what will work until we come up with the Love Rule. One of Jake's postcards has a stack of money on the front. One has a cow. On another card, three old ladies are playing guitars.

We both go back to work and leave with cards of old couples holding hands and little kids kissing, race cars and waterslides, a big question mark, an ear, a telephone, a seagull, an alligator, a bald-headed guy, a smiling face, a frowning face, and everything we think might ever come up.

On the way to the car we pass a withered old man. His straight black hair reaches his waist, and he's wearing a blanket for a vest. He sits cross-legged, strumming a homemade stringed instrument and singing, "Like a Rhinestone Cowboy," over and over—only the first few bars. Maybe that's the extent of his repertoire. I give him the little money I have on me, even though it's soggy. Then I hurry to catch up with Jake.

23

Sunday, instead of finding a church to go to, I lie in bed and read unassigned poetry by Edna St. Vincent Millay and Ann Brontë, who didn't write *Wuthering Heights* or *Jane Eyre* but could put together a great poem. I'm a good enough Christian to feel guilty for not going to church. I'm not a good enough one to actually go.

The afternoon wears on, and the phone score climbs to Jeremy Skittles, eight, Eric Jensen, zero.

I walk back from supper, alone, surprised how much I've missed my roommate. She's still not there when I get back to my room. But the *New Mail* box is showing on my computer. I have another anonymous e-mail. As I click on the message, I can't stop my mind from playing tricks and conjuring up Eric, sitting at the keyboard, hopelessly in love . . . with *me*.

```
:: Dear Mattie ::
I can't tell you how grateful I was to get your
e-mail. Thanks. Sorry I didn't have nerve to
```

meet you at the game. I'm just so attracted to
you, Mattie. (Don't be offended, please.) And
when there's a physical attraction, it can
cloud the other dimensions of a relationship. I
want to know all about you. But if we were
together, I doubt if I could concentrate on
anything except how beautiful you are. So help
me. Will you write back? And tell me all the
things you care about? Let me see how beautiful
you are on the inside.

I guess it's only fair that I go first, right?
I probably care too much about finding the
right person to love. Almost every day I drive
past people who not only don't have love, but
have no roof over their heads, no place to call
home.

He goes on talking about the homeless. It's like this guy can
read my heart. Then the whole mood of the —message changes and
takes me with it.

People are still asking me what I want to be
when I grow up, and yesterday I got the answer.
I'm going to own an airline for pets. You heard
it first, Mattie. The planes will have all
first-class seats, for first-class pets, all
purebred. I'll seat the St. Bernards by the
emergency exits, of course. Police dogs will
handle gate security. We'll serve kitty and
doggie treats in tiny bags, to save money. You
can guess the in-flight movie lineup—<u>101
Dalmatians, Cats and Dogs, Lady and the Tramp.</u>
And instead of jet lag, my Frequent-Flyer
Felines will get pet lag. What do you think?

What do I think? I think I *have* to meet this mystery e-mail man. He may be the only male at Freedom University with an honest-to-goodness sense of humor. I think I'm in love.

By the time Gillian gets back, I've sent Mystery Man the longest e-mail of my life, answering all of his questions with total honesty. Well, almost. And I asked him some tough questions of my own. I want to know what he thinks about relationships, about God, about flocks of birds, and ice on windows.

Gillian and I sit on the floor and start in on the peanut butter cookies her mom sent back with her. I pump her for details about her family. We're laughing hard at the crush Gillian's little brother has on his Sunday School teacher, when the door to our suite mates' room opens, and in walks Naomi. She's blowing on her fingernails, which are too long and perfect to be real.

"Hey, Naomi," Gillian calls. "Is Laura still out on her big date with Super Steve?"

Naomi groans and sits on Gillian's bed. "I told her not to go."

"Why?" I really don't get this part of the Operation Steve strategy.

"Steve the Player showed up an hour late," Naomi explains. "He kept that poor girl waiting and waiting. I thought I'd have to drive her to the ER."

Gillian shakes her head. "Did he say why he was late?"

"Not to me," Naomi answers. "Laura should have sent that boy home. But she didn't. She tripped over herself getting downstairs when he called up."

"Do you really believe Steve showed up late on purpose?" I ask.

"I do," Naomi answers. "I think he knew exactly how our Laura would take it too."

We take turns saying what a loser Steve is. Then we trade stories about rotten guys we've dated. They have a lot more stories than I do, and some are pretty funny. I pop popcorn, and we talk long after the sun goes down, leaving us sitting in the dark.

I'm not sure I've ever talked like this with anybody except

Emma, and it feels nice. "What I want to know is, if ignorance is bliss, why aren't more guys happy?"

"Exactly!" Naomi agrees.

"*And*," I continue, on a roll now, "how can girls talk about what jerks guys are, and then be *so* surprised when guys *act* like jerks?"

Before Naomi can answer and enlighten me, the door opens, and Laura stumbles in.

"I thought I heard voices." Laura's slurring her words. "Why is it so dark in here?"

Gillian gets up and turns on her desk lamp. Then she puts her arm around Laura and leads her over to us. Laura kind of collapses on the floor, laughing. Her hair is messed up.

"Well, *somebody* had a good time," Naomi observes, straightening her roommate's hair.

"Oh, I did!" Laura assures us. She's so eager, she reminds me of Rhett, Emma's Irish setter. "I really, really did have a *wonderful* time." She's dreamy, and more than a little drunk. "Do you think Steve had a wonderful time?" She looks from one of us to the other. "Do you think *he's* wondering if I had a wonderful time?"

"Nope," Naomi answers. "He's eating Doritos and having another beer. That's what they do."

"I'm not asking for much," Laura declares, as if we've accused her of it. "I just want Steve to be there for me!"

I hate that cliché. "What does that mean anyway? Be *where* for you? When?"

"Laura,"—Gillian helps her settle against the bunk, since she's tilting—"I didn't know you drank."

"I don't," Laura says. "But I did."

"No kidding." I sniff and almost gag. She must have spilled her beer because the whole room smells like a Michelob moment. "Unless that magic perfume of Naomi's has Eau de Budweiser in it."

Laura spins around to face me. Then she covers her mouth. She looks like she's going to be sick.

"You okay?" I scoot away.

She stays like that a second, then removes her hand from her mouth. "I'm fine. But I'm really sorry I'm drunk, Mattie."

"You don't have to apologize to *me*," I tell her.

"But I do. I do!" she insists. "You shouldn't have to be around drunks. Not here."

I'm getting a sick feeling in my stomach. "What do you mean, 'not here'?"

Laura doesn't answer.

I catch Naomi and Gillian exchanging looks.

"What?" I demand. But I know. I know that they know.

Laura starts to cry. "I don't want to be a drunk like your mother. I don't want to make you sad, Mattie. I'm a horrible person."

Gillian is staring at her hands.

"Who told you about my mother?" I ask.

"It's nothing, Mattie," Gillian whispers. "Nobody cares. You don't have to—"

"It's Val, isn't it?" But I don't need her to tell me. I know. It's Valerie Ramsey.

I get up so fast I nearly knock Laura over. Without another word, I storm out of our room and charge down the hall to Val's room. It's after midnight, but lights and music come from nearly every room—except Val's. I knock.

No answer.

I knock again, louder. And I keep knocking because I don't know what else to do. My mind is on automatic pilot, fueled by years of venom from Val Ramsey. In Hamilton she never missed an opportunity to bad-mouth my mom. And I'm not letting it happen here. I bang harder.

When the door opens, I'm so surprised I step back. "Listen to me, Val—" I begin.

She squints from her dark room. Her hair is a mess, and she's got her blanket wrapped around her. "What do you want?" There's no fake niceness in her voice.

"What do I want? I want you to keep your big, fat, venomous

mouth shut. That's what I want. Why do you think you have to drag—"

She's not listening to me. She keeps turning back into her room, holding the door open a crack.

"Hey! I'm talking to you!" I yell.

"Okay, okay. Now go away," she hisses.

"I'm not going away until you apologize and promise to shut up about me and about my mother. Do you hear me, Val?"

"What?" She turns back to me again. "Yeah. Whatever."

I stick my foot in her door because I'm afraid she's shutting it. "What's with you?" I try to peer into the room. She's worried about something.

Then a male voice comes from the bed. "Valerie, for crying out loud. Apologize and come back to bed."

I'm stunned. I can't see the guy in Val's bed, but I definitely heard him. "Well, what do we have here?" I ask.

"We have nothing here." Val pushes on the door.

"You don't think so? Hmm . . . I wonder what Jake thinks. You know, I think I'll go ask him."

"Don't you dare, Mattie!"

I smile. I got her. And I can't wait to tell Jake.

I run to Jake's dorm and fly up the stairs, two at a time.

When I tap on Jake's door, Carson opens it. "Mattie? Hi! You look great."

I was counting on getting Jake by himself. "Hi, Carson. Jake around?"

Jake appears. "What's up, Matt?"

"I need to talk to you, Jake."

Carson opens the door all the way. "Come on in. I need you to talk to Jake too."

"Carson." Jake punches him in the shoulder.

"What?" I can tell they've been arguing about something.

"Your old buddy here wants to quit basketball," Carson explains.

"Jake!" I exclaim. "You can't quit. You haven't even started yet." This is exactly what Emma and I were afraid of. The rush for Jake was in getting on the team.

"I didn't say I was quitting," Jake insists. "Just thinking about it."

"And he's the best freshman on the team," Carson continues. "Coach likes him. The guys like him. I don't get it."

"Penultimate," I conclude.

Carson frowns. "Pen-what?"

"Give it a rest, Matt," Jake begs.

I ignore him and explain to Carson the Penultimate Moment theory—how Jake lives for the anticipation of things, then loses interest the minute he gets what he wants.

"Dude!" Carson pats Jake on the back. "That is Jake here all over."

"I don't appreciate the psychoanalysis." Jake rubs the back of his neck. "I'm just not enjoying basketball as much as I thought I would."

"Penultimate," Carson repeats.

"Back off," Jake pleads. "Okay. If I promise not to quit yet, will you guys leave me alone? Anyway, that's not why you came over here. What's up, Matt?"

I study Jake's face, the tiny lines at the corners of his eyes. He's really been struggling with this. It's like he's lost his love for basketball. How can I tell him about Val? I know he doesn't love Val, but she's been his security blanket for a long time. "I need a moon check," I say at last.

"A what?" Carson's brow wrinkles.

Jake shuts off his computer and heads toward the door. "Carson, if anybody calls for me, take a message."

I'm grateful that Jake still honors moon checks. No questions. No hesitation.

We find a place by the basketball courts and sit on the grass, which is dry as desert. Nobody else is around, although bursts of voices come from the dorm. In and out of the gray, wispy clouds floats a sliver of moon. It's enough. I can feel my muscles relax, and my mind follows suit.

As we sit there in silence, the same thing happens to me that happened at the ocean. It's like something in me begins talking to God, without my even planning it. *Thanks for this, God. Why can't I remember you're this close all the time?*

After a while Jake and I talk. I'm not even sure who starts. But Jake tells me about some girl he met at a frat party he and Carson went to. And I tell him about Jeremy Skittles and Eric Jensen. Finally I tell him about my mystery e-mailer, although I'm careful not to tell him I think it's Eric.

"Whoever this mystery man is, Jake, it's like he knows me. Don't say it—it's crazy. Sounds like a made-for-TV movie, right? Or one of Val's romance novels? But this guy is right about how hard it is to get to know anybody through dating."

Jake turns and smiles down at me—smiles, not laughs.

I change the subject. "So what's going on with Stella?"

Jake stares at the clouds that hide the moon. "I don't know, Matt. Maybe Stella is out of my reach."

"Nobody's out of your reach, Jake. Except maybe Val—too far down for you."

He shoots me a scolding look that can't hide his dimple.

I have got to keep Jake away from Val, even if it means shoving him into the arms of Stella. "Promise me you won't give up on Stella, Jake. Not yet."

Monday night, Jake and I take up where we left off. He brings the postcards to our midnight meeting, and we head for the beach. My idea.

Turns out to be a great idea. The beach is deserted, compared to Saturday—black ocean and black sky, with cold, white stars cutting through and the silvery moon leaving a rippled streak on the water. Waves lap the shore, making a kind of sea music against the sand. Seagulls cry softly in the background. A cool breeze blows my hair across my face.

"Wild Scottish Mattie." Jake brushes back my tangles.

We find a place in the sand and lean against a brushy dune. A few stragglers still walk the beach. I breathe deeply, inhaling air that smells like the moon would smell if it could.

Jake yawns. "So, how was your Eric today?"

"My Eric doesn't seem to notice *my* existence. I saw him twice, and he breezed right by me. I can't stop thinking about him, Jake."

"Tell me about it."

"Stella on the brain?"

He nods.

"Well, speaking of the lovely Miss Stella, guess who I ate lunch with today?"

Jake sits up straight. "You're kidding. What did you say, Matt?"

"Girl talk. I did manage to put in a good word for you, though." It hadn't been easy. At first, Stella hadn't known who I was talking about. When I described Jake and said he was in her logic class, she remembered him. But she didn't seem anxious to know more. "I told her you were a guy from back home—very intelligent, good sense of humor—and that you were in her logic class."

"And that's when she got up and walked away?" Jake settles back against the dune.

"No."

"It's no use, Matt. Professor Nettles makes me look like an idiot. I can't get past that with Stella."

"You want to try not giving up on the girl until *after* you've won her? We're still in the Penultimate Phase here, Jake."

"Funny." He doesn't smile.

This Nettles prof must be something to get Jake so discouraged. I think I'd like to meet this guy.

"I can't stop thinking about her, Matt," he admits.

"I know."

We lie there, lost in our own thoughts.

Finally Jake sits up and brings out the bag of postcards. "So, what's the Love Rule for this week?"

I sit up, cross-legged, and pull out my pen. We toss around a couple of ideas but keep coming back to the way we can't stop thinking about Eric and Stella. I finger through the postcards and settle for the one of a bald-headed guy with question marks and exclamation points coming out of his head. Then I write,

LOVE RULE #2
Love controls your mind and makes you think constantly about the one you love.

We address the card to

Auntie Em
Hamilton, Missouri 64644

I've known Dewy Blackburn, the postman, forever. He'll have a good laugh, then take it directly to Emma.

Jake walks me to my dorm, even though I tell him he doesn't need to.

"I better take the postcard," I offer when we reach the steps. "You'll forget to mail it."

"True." He hands it over. "Night."

Bob's wife, June, is vacuuming the lobby when I walk in. I stop and visit with her for a few minutes, then head up.

I reach the stairwell, and a flash of red catches my eye. I turn to see Val Ramsey, sitting in the darkest corner of the lobby with her football boyfriend. The two of them are going at it like bait worms in a bucket.

I make a U-turn and breeze by them, pretending to only now notice my old friend, Val. "Oh, Valerie! Hey. Listen, I got that cold sore medicine you wanted. You can come down to my room and get it later. Night."

I don't sleep much Monday night. Big news. I'm setting some kind of no-sleep record. I should offer myself up to medical science. Lying in bed, I have too much time to think. I think about Mom and wonder how she's getting along. I think about Eric. And I think about the lousy logic professor making Jake feel stupid. How illogical is that?

By the time it's morning, I've made up my mind. I get up and dressed. I even put on makeup.

"You don't have a class this early, do you?" Gillian yawns from her bunk.

"I'm going to logic class," I announce.

"You don't have a logic class."

"I do today." While I brush my hair, I fill her in on Jake's problem with Stella and Professor Nettles.

"I can see why you want to help your friend, Mattie," Gillian says. "But what can you do?"

"I've got a couple of ideas. I'll tell you all about it when I get back."

I time my walk across campus so that I arrive right after logic class starts. Jake is sitting in the middle of the room, next to Stella. Without acknowledging Jake, I take the empty seat directly in front of him. Then I give Professor Nettles my best smile and pull out a Southern accent. It's not that hard. Most people in California think Missourians have Southern accents anyway. "I apologize for my rude tardiness, Professor."

He smiles back in a way that makes me think Jake could be right about him. Nettles isn't much older than we are. "We're glad to have you join us, Miss—" He waits for me to fill in the blank.

"Miss Guardian. Angel Guardian."

Behind me, I hear Stella whisper, "I thought her name was Mattie."

Jake whispers something to her, but I can't make it out.

"Guardian, Angel," Professor Nettles repeats. "I feel safer already." The only other person he looks at is Stella. It's clear he's performing for an audience of two.

"Thank y'all," I drawl.

"Well, since you missed my introductory talk last week," Nettles begins, "I'd like to welcome you to logic class with a quote from Samuel Johnson that illustrates the environment of my classes—with the freedom to speak as you wish, as long as it is logical. 'Every man has a right to utter what he thinks truth.'"

I've heard this quote before. "Excuse me," I interrupt.

"Yes, Ms. Guardian." He's still smiling, but you can tell he hates the interruption.

"Didn't y'all quote the rest of that line from Samuel Johnson?" I ask innocently.

"The rest of it?"

"Uh-huh. If I'm not mistaken, the whole quote goes, 'Every man has a right to utter what he thinks truth, and every other man has a right to knock him down for it.'" It really is the whole quote. I'm not making it up.

A couple of my fellow classmates chuckle, but there's no freedom in this class. They don't laugh long.

"Thank you, Ms. Guardian. Now, where were we in our last

discussion?" Nettles checks his notes. "Yes. We discussed the ethics of the man who yells 'Fire!' in a crowded movie theater. Does anyone have anything to add before we move on?"

I stretch my arms above my head, like I'm yawning. I hope Jake is paying attention and has the guts to play along with me. Casually I sign, *Ask him if it's ethical to yell "Movie!" in a crowded fire station.*

Jake must have raised his hand, because Professor Nettles, disbelief written on his face, says, "Mr. Jackson, you have a question?"

"I was wondering," Jake begins with the perfect serious pitch, "is it ethical for a man to yell 'Movie!' in a crowded fire station?"

Several of us brave laughter. Professor Nettles isn't one of us.

"Since you're so willing to contribute to our class today, Mr. Jackson, would you be so kind as to give us an example of Aristotelian logic, a syllogistic example?"

Before I can sign for him, Jake answers, "I don't understand."

Professor Nettles sighs dramatically. "I see that, like Aristotle, I am misunderstood by the rabble. So it is with genius."

Now I sign fast.

Jake reads my fingers and speaks. "The fact that people don't understand you doesn't make you a genius, does it? That doesn't seem logical."

The crowd murmurs. I get the feeling they would love to see Jake take down this prof.

Professor Nettles stiffens. "Mr. Jackson, do you have an example for us of Aristotelian logic, or don't you?"

I stick both hands behind my back and move my fingers to sign, *I am a nobody.*

It takes Jake a minute. He's going to have to trust me on this one. Finally he says, "I am a nobody."

I sign the rest, and Jake takes it from there. "Nobody is perfect. Therefore, I am perfect."

I lead the applause, but almost everybody else joins in.

If Nettles were a cartoon, smoke would be coming out his ears. "Mr. Jackson, I don't know if you're the most ignorant student I've ever had, or merely the most apathetic."

I fake messing with my hair and sign, *Don't know. Don't care.*

Jake echoes me, in answer to Nettles' calling him ignorant and apathetic. Stella gets it and laughs out loud.

I see Nettles eyeing Stella as she laughs. He changes tactics and forces a smile. "Very good, Mr. Jackson. Perhaps I've misspoken where you're concerned."

I sign, and Jake doesn't miss a beat. "Wasn't it Sophocles who said, 'It is a terrible thing to speak well and be wrong'?"

Nettles' mouth twitches. Then he turns to the board and starts writing.

I want to glance back at Jake and give him the thumbs-up, but I don't dare.

The rest of the hour Nettles leaves Jake alone. He even calls on other students to answer questions. And Jake, feeling himself again, raises his hand and answers something that came from the assigned readings. Nettles doesn't give him any grief about it either.

When class is over, I turn to see if Jake wants to go celebrate with me. But he's talking to Stella.

"You seem to have bounced back in this class," Stella is saying.

Jake isn't responding. I can't believe Jake Jackson is tongue-tied. I clear my throat, but act like I'm fixing my belt. Then I sign, *There's an old Japanese proverb that says, "Fall seven times, stand up eight—you win."*

Jake delivers the line with perfect timing and gets the golden laugh of Stella for his reward.

I slip out of the room.

Mission accomplished.

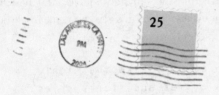

25

```
:: Mattie ::
You guys outdid yourselves on the postcard.
Great Love Rule how you can't stop thinking
about the one you love. Okay. My turn. Check
out Psalm 139:17.

Love, Emma
```

I print out Emma's e-mail, which arrives on Thursday. Then Gillian helps me look up the verse, and we read it together. "How precious are your thoughts about me, O God! They are innumerable! I can't even count them; they outnumber the grains of sand! And when I wake up in the morning, you are still with me!"

"Makes me think of the beach Jake took me to," I comment.

"That's a lot of thoughts, huh?" Gillian picks up my Bible and reads the verse again. She flips Bible pages until she gets to Psalm 40. Then she reads the last verse: "'As for me, I am poor and needy, but the Lord is thinking about me right now.'"

I read it silently for myself. "Emma would love that."

"I like this Emma of yours. Think she'll come to Freedom U next fall?"

"I don't know, Gillian." And before I know it, I'm telling her all about Emma's disease.

All next week in the English department Eric stubbornly refuses to notice me. But I've been getting more mystery e-mails. And in each e-mail, there's a quote that makes me feel this guy knows me inside out.

On Tuesday, he quotes Lord Byron.

```
She walks in Beauty, like the night
Of cloudless climes and starry skies,
And all that s best of dark and bright
Meet in her aspect and her eyes.
```

Wednesday, it's Keats.

```
I cannot exist without you I am forgetful
of every thing but seeing you again my Life
seems to stop there I can see no further.
You have absorb'd me.
```

Thursday, he writes,

```
Whatever our souls are made of, yours and
mine are the same.
```

It's Emily Brontë, whom I love. And I'm so moved, I almost believe him. It scares me how strong my feelings are growing.

On Friday, I think he's hinting that we should meet. I want to, so much. But when I write back that he should ask me in person—there's still a chance it's not Eric—he quotes John Dryden.

```
Pains of love be sweeter far
Than all other pleasures are.
```

I can picture Eric putting those cute air quotes around "pains."

I answer each e-mail, and we have honest discussions. We talk about God—he's afraid to take the "leap of faith" and discover it won't hold him. I tell him that I've made that leap but can't seem to get comfortable on the side of faith. It's too scary to need someone, even God. We talk about love and about finding the right person and being the right person and how hard it is to date.

Eric, however, does *not* ask me out in person—unlike Jeremy Skittles, who continues to ask me in all available media—phone, note passed in class, face-to-face in hallways.

Jake and I talk once during the week, when he calls to thank me for my logic class performance. Nettles has stopped harassing him, and he's trying to get up the courage to ask Stella out. It's a nice conversation, until he lets it slip that he's talked to Val.

"Jake!"

"*She* called *me*," he explains. "She's going through a rough time."

"Listen, Jake." I'm thinking this is the time to tell him about Val and her boyfriend. But Jake must sense something coming because he hangs up before I can go through with it.

Monday night Jake drives us to the beach for our postcard assignment. This time we both walk barefoot in the sand. It makes me think of Emma's verse. "Did you know that each grain of sand is a thought from God about *you*?" I ask.

Jake grins. "Sounds like Emma's been sending you e-mail verses too."

"Isn't she great, Jake? Does she have the whole Bible memorized? Because she has a verse for everything."

"I don't know if she has the Bible memorized, but she reads it all the time." He's quiet for a minute. "I'm not sure I'd be so tight with God if I were in Emma's shoes."

I stare up at him to see if he means this. Moonlight brushes half of Jake's face, but I can't make out his expression. "You mean her lupus?"

He nods.

"Emma told me once that she thinks she's gotten so tight with God *because* of her lupus, not in spite of it."

Jake doesn't say anything. We settle against our sand dune.

"I wish I believed as much as Emma," I continue. "What about you, Jake?"

Jake shakes his head slowly. "I've thought about it. But I don't think it's for me."

"Why not?" I press.

He shrugs. "If it worked, I'd probably get tired of it, right?" He turns and grins at me. "Penultimate."

We're quiet awhile. Then Jake breaks the silence. "How are you and the graduate getting along?"

"We're not," I admit. "I've done everything but voodoo on the phone, and he still hasn't called to ask me out. Good ol' Jeremy hasn't quit calling, though. How about you and the lovely Ms. Stella?"

"I got up nerve to call her, but I just got her voice mail. She hasn't called me back."

"I'll bet good ol' Val has called back, though," I venture.

Jake grins, so I know I'm right.

He dumps out the sack of postcards and spreads them over the sand until he finds the one he's looking for. "What do you think?" He holds up a picture of an old-fashioned telephone, the kind with a wooden box and a black funnel in the center. The receiver is dangling from the side.

"Perfect," I answer, pulling out my pen. I turn over the card and write,

LOVE RULE #3
The one you don't want to call you will always call, and the one you're dying to have call you won't.

Jake takes the pen and scribbles.

So, maybe the secret to love is not really liking the person you want to love you.

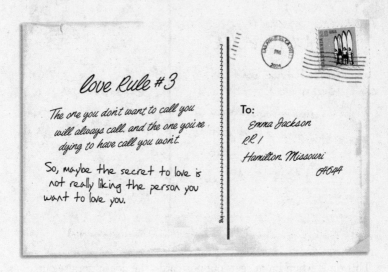

love Rule #3

The one you don't want to call you will always call, and the one you're dying to have call you won't.

So, maybe the secret to love is not really liking the person you want to love you.

To:
Emma Jackson
RR 1
Hamilton, Missouri
64644

In the pile of postcards, I see the cow card. A black-and-white cow is stretching her neck over a barbed-wire fence to eat grass on the other side. "Jake, think Emma could use two cards this week?"

Jake laughs, and I know he knows what I'm thinking. He takes the pen from me and writes on the back of the cow card,

Bonus LOVE RULE
We want what we don't, or can't, have in love.

Now it's my turn to take the pen from Jake and add:

So, if you want someone to like you, stay on the other side of the fence.

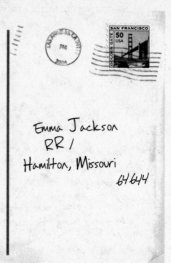

Bonus LOVE RULE

We want what we don't, or can't, have in love.

So, if you want someone to like you, stay on the other side of the fence.

Emma Jackson
RR 1
Hamilton, Missouri
64644

This time, when Emma gets our postcards, she doesn't praise our insightful comments. She just thanks us for sending two cards in one week. And she sends me on a Bible hunt for two verses—"The reason you don't have what you want is that you don't ask God for it" (James 4:2) and "Keep on asking, and you will be given what you ask for" (Matthew 7:7).

That night I fall asleep asking God for love.

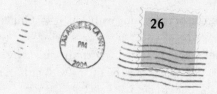

26

Friday night Naomi bursts into the room while Gillian and I are studying. No date here.

"Heads up," Naomi declares. "I need your help."

Gillian gasps. "*You* need *our* help?"

"I'll handle this, Gillian." I swivel around in my desk chair. "Naomi probably needs dating and relationship advice. Sure. Go ahead, Naomi. Dr. Mattie is in."

"Funny." She looks around for a place to sit. She can't find one, so she leans on the bunks. "Listen, this is serious. Laura is in bad, bad shape. We need to help her."

"Steve still hasn't called her back?" Gillian asks.

"Steve is a stupidhead," I pronounce.

Naomi frowns. "Where do you get these words?"

"Missouri. But it seems to apply in California. *Stupidhead* has always been my favorite term. Emma, my friend from back home, thought it up when she was five. But you could also go with 'buckethead' or 'swamphead' if you want to sound more grown up."

Naomi turns to my roommate. "Didn't I tell you from day one

that Stevie was a player? At least I'm keeping our Laura from totally embarrassing herself by stalking the guy."

I know for a fact that Laura has called Steve behind Naomi's back—more than once. She sneaks over and uses our phone. She even leaves messages, which breaks one of Naomi's cardinal rules.

Gillian closes her book. "What can we do to help?"

"We need to get that girl back in circulation—tonight." Naomi stares at us.

"I could go to a movie or something with you, if—" Gillian starts.

"A movie?" Naomi sounds horrified. "With the girls? Not what I had in mind. You don't meet guys by sitting with girls in a dark theater. We're taking our girl *out*."

Gillian turns back to her book. "Sorry. I gave up hunting guys the day I met Michael."

"I thought you'd say that." Naomi turns to me. She looks a little like Catwoman as she closes in on me. "You could use some circulating yourself, Mattie."

I'd rather have open-heart surgery than circulate. "Thanks, but no thanks, Naomi."

"Some friend you are. Poor Laura is so down. You've seen her. I canceled my Friday night date to do this for her, and you can't even be bothered to—?"

"Okay, okay." She got me with the "poor Laura" routine. And Naomi's right. I've been worried about Laura. She's not eating right, and she walks around with red eyes from crying over Steve. "You win."

Naomi makes me change clothes while she grabs Laura from next door. Then Laura and I follow our leader to the land of circulation.

Naomi drives and ends up in the dark parking lot of a dive called the 21 Club. She shuts off the engine.

"Naomi," I object, "you don't seriously expect Laura to find Mr. Right in there, do you?"

"Who needs Mr. Right?" she counters. "Laura needs Mr. Right Now." She shoves us out of her car.

"I'm only 17, you know," I remind her as we walk under the 21 sign.

Naomi digs in her purse. "Not a problem." She deals Laura and me fake IDs. The picture on mine looks like Elvis's mother.

"This doesn't even look like me," Laura complains. "And it says I'm 25."

"Trust me." Naomi leads the way. "I know the bouncer."

She walks us past the big man stationed at the door. He doesn't even look at our IDs because he can't keep his eyes off Naomi.

We cross the threshold into the 21 Club, and music blasts us with the force of a tidal wave. Laura says something, but I can't hear what. The room smells like sweat and beer, mixed with smoke. This is a glorified bar, with cheesy tables scattered across the grimy, tiled floor. In the back there's a real bar, with wobbly stools and a TV you can't even hear because of the crowd noise. The room is packed.

"Where do you want to sit?" Laura screams.

"In the car?" I suggest.

"What?" Laura shouts.

"With my back to the wall, where I can see the exit!" I shout back.

Naomi is silently shopping the room. Her gaze mows down packs of guys, systematically surveying from left to right, right to left. She glides to a table in the center of the room, and Laura and I follow, like lost children.

I hope Jake hasn't taken Stella to a place like this. Tonight is his first date with the Wonder Blonde. He called me three times to ask what he should wear, where he should take her, and if I'd learned anything else about her that would help him keep the conversation going. I tried to talk him into getting tickets for Freedom U's production of *Annie*, but I don't know if he did it or not.

Laura looks to Naomi when we're sitting at the table. "What if Steve sees me here?"

"That would be great!" Naomi insists. "Uh-oh. Heads up, girls. We've got a live one heading our way."

✳

Slick

I scope out the crowd, then spit on my hand and slick back my hair. I could have had a date tonight. But I felt like cruising. I gaze around the 21 Club and can tell I'm the best-looking guy here. Not bragging. Just the facts, ma'am. So I can legally go for the best-looking girl here, right?

And there she is, sitting at a table in the middle of the floor. Actually, it might be a tie. This brunette, with long hair and a great bod, is hanging with an Asian chick, who's not bad herself. Can't go wrong at that table. I head for them, still not sure which girl I'll choose. But a big hulk of a guy, with cowboy boots, moves in and pulls up a chair next to the Asian girl.

I veer toward the brunette. She's even prettier close up, with bright blue eyes. I smile at her and keep walking. Then, as if I hadn't been headed for her all along, I turn around and walk back, locking her with my eyes. "Hey," I say, voice low. "Do you believe in love at first sight? Or should I walk by again?"

"Good one," she answers, but not with feeling. I have my work cut out with this one.

"Come on, Laura," the Asian girl tells the girl who's sulking at the table with them. "Let's get something to drink with Hank. Looks like Mattie's busy."

They leave for the bar, and I take the seat next to the brunette. "So, Maddie, is it? Kyle. Come here often?"

"Too often," she answers.

"I know what you mean." I can't believe I've never noticed this one before.

"Sorry. I'm really not good company. I'm . . . not into this." She gives me this sexy smile, and I know she's playing me.

"Don't apologize, Maddie." I pat her hand, then leave my hand there, on top of hers.

She pulls back her hand. "It's *Mattie*. And I wasn't apologizing—just explaining."

"Hey." I push away from the table. "No explanations needed.

This really isn't my scene either. Why don't we get out of here?" I stand up. "Let's take a little drive. Just you and me."

She stays seated.

"Come on, Maddie. My car's right outside." I point to my Humvee, parked right in front, where everybody can see it. That's usually all I need.

"Is that yours?" she asks. "The one in the handicapped zone?"

I shrug. "Yeah. There were five spots, none of them used. I mean, who's going to come here in a wheelchair, right?"

"It's still reserved for the handicapped," she insists.

"So?"

"So, the last time I looked, stupidity wasn't an official handicap." She gets up and walks to the bar, where her friends are drinking.

Probably doesn't like men.

Mattie

"So what happened?" Naomi demands. She's sitting on Hank's lap. We've reclaimed our table, but there aren't enough chairs to go around. "Well? How did you lose him, Mattie? He was cute."

"Trust me, Naomi." I struggle to keep my temper checked. "Cute isn't everything."

"It's a lot." Naomi strokes Hank's thick, curly dark hair. Hank grins sheepishly.

"Have a beer," Laura suggests, draining hers. "It'll make you feel better."

"Yeah. Like the last two times you've hurled in our bathroom? That kind of 'feel better,' I can do without, thanks." The music is pounding in my head with a monotone beat. People definitely don't come here for the music. "You know you don't have to do this, Laura. You're—"

"Hey there," yells a male, inches from my ear.

Naomi elbows me. "Looks like you snagged another one."

✳

The Pickup Artist

Cruising bars is an art, and I am an artist. It's not only an art. It's a science. So I guess I'm a scientist too. I should write that one down.

Stage One—Surveillance. I scan the room, checking who's here. I sure don't want to zero in on one and then see a better one off in a corner somewhere. I make another round before making my pick. The "pick" comes before the "pickup."

Got her. A black-haired beauty is staring around the room like she's anxious to find the right guy. Her friends are pretty cute, but she's the one. She wins. Stage One is complete.

Stage Two—The Pickup Line. I've got a million of them. No sweat. I breeze by her table and act like I'm seeing her for the first time. "Somebody, call the cops! It's illegal to look that good!" This line never fails me. It's an art. Right line for the right girl.

She smiles at me. One point for the Brewster.

"Abel Brewster." I give her my profile and ease against her table.

"Abel Brewster," she begins, "I'm sure you're a really great guy, but—"

"Ah, so my reputation has preceded me."

"—but I'm so not interested."

"That's okay," I assure her. "I'm interested enough for the both of us."

She takes a deep breath. "Please go away."

"Whoa!" I exclaim. I know she's playing hard to get. I mimic licking my finger, then touch her arm. "Ow! Sizzling hot. I'm not going anywhere. I'll always be there for you."

"Seriously, you better leave. It's going to get ugly in about two seconds."

I turn to the mousy girl, who's frowning over her beer. She's kinda cute. "So does your friend here have a license to kill, or what?" I ask the mousy one.

The black-haired babe snaps, "I don't have a license to kill. But I *do* have my learner's permit. Go." She stands up. "No. Never mind. *I'll* go."

She strides away, and I'm sure she wants me to come running after her. But no female, not even one who looks like that, is worth that much effort. I take the now empty seat next to the mousy girl. "So, what's your name, good-looking? How about I touch up that beer for you?"

∗

Mattie

In my head, which is pounding with the one-stick drumbeat, I try to compose my next e-mail to Emma.

Em,
I think I know what hell's like. And people come here on purpose!
I would rather remain dateless the rest of my life than return to the
21 Club one more time.

If it weren't for the fact that Jake's out on his first date with Wonder Blonde Stella, I'd call him to come rescue me. But I can't do that, not on his first date. So I talk to God instead. *So, God, I don't want to be here. I don't know where I'm going to find love, but I think we both agree it won't be here.* It's kind of cool that God's here to talk to, even though I know we'd both rather be anyplace else.

Out of the corner of my eye, I see movement. Someone is heading straight toward me. *Okay, God. Don't let me lose my temper and flatten this guy.*

∗

One-Track

It's no secret. People come here for one reason—they want to get laid. I'm no different. I've had enough to drink tonight that I could sleep with almost any girl in this room. I just want to score. I'm tired of hearing my frat brothers brag about their weekends. Well, tonight is mine.

I look for a girl by herself and find her—very cute, dark hair, nervous-acting. I saunter over to her. This is the part I hate, the first word. Then I hate the second part too, where you have to act like you're interested in what they're saying. "Hi!"

179

She looks like she's ready to bite my head off. "That's it? 'Hi'?"

I shrug. Maybe this wasn't the best choice. "Haven't seen you around here before."

"Because I haven't been around here before," she snaps.

I'll give it one more try, but there are plenty of fish in the sea tonight. "Want me to get you something to drink?"

"I'm 17."

Great. What's the legal age to sleep with somebody anyway? I should know, but I can't think straight. Too many beers. "I meant, like a Coke or something." Her face softens, and I think maybe I can pull this out after all. "I was going to get myself a Coke," I lie. "Want one?"

"I'm sorry." She's really pretty when her face isn't so hard. "I guess this place is getting to me. And I thought you were—Never mind. Let's get that Coke."

Yes! We walk to the bar and sit down. I order two Cokes, and we start the small talk. I let her do most of the talking, and I nod and make interested noises. I wonder how long I have to do it. Not that it's so bad really. Part of me thinks, if I hadn't come here to get laid, I might even ask her out. "Hamilton sounds cool." I take a swig of Coke.

"Are you really 20?" she asks.

It doesn't seem so important, since she's only 17. "Eighteen. I kind of stretched the truth earlier."

"Stretch the truth far enough, and it will snap back at you." But she's grinning when she says this.

I laugh. I like her sense of humor. But that's not why I'm here. I think it's time to make my move. "Mattie, since I'm new in town, how about giving me directions . . . to your place?"

"To *my* place?"

"Yeah. There's no privacy in the Beta house. Is your roommate cool?"

She stands up slowly, and for a minute, I'm afraid she's going to hit me.

180

Mattie

I get away from the "Your-place-or-mine" cliché as fast as I can. For a minute, I actually thought I could have a decent conversation here.

Laura's still at the table with the License-to-Kill guy. I've got to get out of here, but I don't see Naomi anywhere. Finally I give up and join Laura. "Laura, I have to go back. Where's Naomi?"

"Go?" Laura looks like she's had too many beers. "It's early."

"Laura, tell me where Naomi is."

"She left."

"Left? She can't leave!"

"She did. With Hank. She said we could find our own way home," Laura explains.

"I'll take you home," her new friend volunteers.

This night is a total nightmare. Panic rises in my stomach.

"Your friend looks really scared," Laura's new fella cleverly observes. "How come?"

"How come?" I repeat. "How about *acousticophobia*, fear of noise? Or *melophobia*, fear of music, this music? Or maybe it's my *macrophobia*, fear of being kept waiting forever? Or how about this? *Ochlophobia*—I'm afraid of mobs. Take your pick!"

"Easy." He looks pretty scared himself now.

I turn to Laura. "Do you have your cell?"

She reaches into her purse and hands me her phone. I dial Jake's cell, hoping I can hear him over the noise. It rings and rings and rings, and I'm terrified his voice mail will pick up.

Finally I hear Jake. "Hello? Hello?"

"Just a minute! I have to get outside!" I feel like a linebacker as I elbow my way to the door and burst into semi-fresh air. "Jake!"

"Matt, are you okay?"

"Sort of. Jake, where are you?"

"In the car. What's the matter? Where are you? I can hardly hear you."

"I'm in hell. They call it 21."

I hear Jake repeat this information to Stella. "Mattie's at 21." I can't hear Stella's response.

Then he's back on the phone. "We'll be right there, Matt. Hang on."

Twenty minutes and almost as many pickup attempts later, Jake's old Ford pulls up. I run to it and jump into the backseat. "I am *so* sorry, you guys! Stella, forgive me. I wouldn't have interrupted your date for anything that wasn't life threatening."

She laughs. "Believe me. I wouldn't have let Jake leave you here, even if he'd wanted to. My roommate went last week, and she said it was horrible."

"What were you doing there, Matt?" Jake steers around a group of smoking girls.

"Naomi talked me into going, to cheer up Laura. Then Naomi left with some guy. Hank. No fooling. That was his name. And I felt like raw meat strung up for a pack of wolves. I tried to get Laura to leave with me, but she wouldn't."

Jake laughs. "So how was the hunting, Matt?"

I plop back in the seat and fasten my seat belt. "They should all be extinct."

"We want details." Stella turns around to face me. "That's your fare. Tell!"

So I launch into the stories. Stella almost chokes, laughing. Jake laughs so hard, I'm afraid he'll drive off the road.

"I'm not kidding," I sum up. "It would have been refreshing to have a guy simply walk up and ask me what a girl like me was doing in a joint like this."

Jake takes the campus exit. We're headed right by Albert's. "Jake, can we—?"

But before I can finish asking, Jake pulls over and hands me a pack of Snickers bars from the glove compartment. "Make it fast, Matt."

I exchange hellos with Albert and his two friends, who seem to like Jake's candy bars better than my granola bars. Then I race back to the car. "Thanks, you guys. Seriously, thanks for everything."

"We're just going to get something to eat, Mattie." Stella smiles at me. "Why don't you come with us?" She sounds like she means it. Most dates would hate me about now.

"That's really cool of you, Stella," I answer. "But all I want is a good night's sleep."

Jake chuckles. I know he knows I won't get one.

I wave as they pull away from my dorm. I didn't expect to like Stella. I'm happy for Jake. But something's gnawing at me, and I have to fight it off and not let myself think about why I feel this way.

I turn and run up the stairs to my room. Gillian's left me a note telling me she's gone home for the night.

I take a shower and wash the smell of the 21 Club out of my hair.

The rest of the night I lie awake and try to decide which is worse—being in a room with a crowd of strangers, or being in a room with nobody but me.

Monday, postcard night, Jake and I settle into our spot on the beach. Then he fills me in on his first date with Stella, the parts I didn't see firsthand.

"I really like her, Jake," I comment when he's done.

"Yeah. Me too."

"You don't sound that enthused though."

"I guess it wasn't as romantic as I thought it would be," he admits.

It's so Jake. Nothing ever lives up. "Give her a chance, Jake."

"I will. We're going out next weekend. I just wish . . ."

His voice trails off, but I know what he's thinking. Dating is nothing like in the movies, and neither is love.

We finally agree on a postcard with a single musical note on the front. I turn it over and write,

LOVE RULE #4
The trouble with love in the real world is that there's no background music.

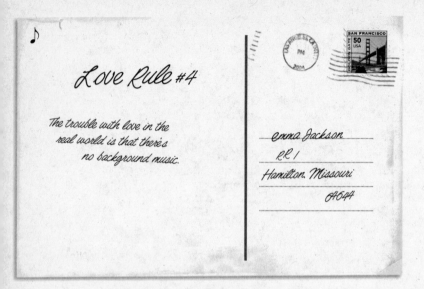

Love Rule #4

*The trouble with love in the
real world is that there's
no background music.*

emma Jackson
RR 1
Hamilton, Missouri
64644

A couple days later Gillian and I are eating lunch with T.C. and one of her friends when we hear, "Congratulations, Stella!"

"Yeah, Stella. Way to go!"

I turn around, and it's Jake's Stella all right. She's beaming. She's wearing a pink tank dress and looks gorgeous.

I wave her over, and she sits down with us. "What's everybody congratulating you for?" I ask.

T.C. frowns at me. "Don't you know anything, girl? Stella's up for homecoming."

I smile at Stella. "Cool!"

"I was so surprised," Stella admits. "There are as many freshmen nominated as there are seniors. Most votes gets homecoming queen, and the next four are on homecoming court. I'm not even sure how many are running. But it ought to be fun."

"You'll win," Gillian promises, finishing her milk.

I agree. We all do.

When I get back to the dorm, there's an e-mail from Emma.

:: Mattie ::
Just got your postcard—a great one! No
background music, huh? Wish you could be here.
If a Missouri fall isn't background music for
love, I don't know what is. Today I walked in
leaves that were seven shades of brown, and
that one shade of burgundy that only God makes
right. Remember when Val tried to dye her hair
that weird red shade? Anyway, the leaves
crackled (True, I couldn't hear them. But you
told me what they sound like). Above me, the
oaks were still clinging to their leaves so
they could rustle and wave in the wind. It made
me think how hard it was for me to let go of
you and Jake, but how rich our lives are
because you're there and I'm here (even though
I miss you both like crazy!).

Wish I could send you the smell of our front
yard when Dad burned leaves, then tossed in
evergreen branches. Maybe love has a background
smell?

But if it's music you're after, check out
1 Corinthians 13, Mattie. Verse 1 talks about
"a loud gong or a clanging cymbal." Sounds like
the 21 Club to me.

Ever Em

I'm still reading 1 Corinthians 13 when Gillian walks in. She
peeks over my shoulder to see what I'm reading.

"Mmmm . . . the 'love chapter,' Michael's favorite."

"I'm thinking I can steal some of these love rules if Jake and I
get hard up one Monday night." I've told Gillian all about the postcard assignment Emma gave Jake and me.

"Good idea," she agrees. Then she recites a couple of the love verses she and Michael memorized together. "'Love is patient and kind. Love is not jealous or boastful or proud or rude. Love does not demand its own way. Love is not irritable, and it keeps no record of when it has been wronged. It is never glad about injustice but rejoices whenever the truth wins out. Love never gives up, never loses faith, is always hopeful, and endures through every circumstance.'"

I close my eyes and listen to Gillian. And what I think of is Eric, my mystery e-mailer. He's been patient—more patient than I am. His e-mails are kind. Okay. So he's kind of rude in person, ignoring me, but I understand and vow not to keep a record of wrongs.

When Gillian finishes, I wonder if Eric will ever come through with the "truth" part of love and tell me he's my mystery e-mailer. And I wonder how long I can keep the faith and hang on to hope.

Eric stays in hiding the rest of the week. I manage to run into him a couple times at work, but he's always in a hurry. Yet he keeps e-mailing almost every night.

When the weekend rolls around, I'm dateless. Again. Even Jeremy has given up on me.

Naomi drags Laura to the bar Friday night, but she couldn't drag me there with a team of Clydesdales.

Monday night Jake and I change strategies and meet early on campus for research. We catch each other by the Flying Squirrel and find a good spot to observe couples. Jake's brought sandwiches, so we eat and spy. Emma, Jake, and I used to people-watch all the time.

"Okay. I'll start." I motion to a couple who could model for Eddie Bauer. They're dressed in campus outdoorsy threads—khaki shorts and boots, with tees and vests. "They've only had one date. She is totally crazy about him and has written her best friend back home in Northern California that she's found 'the one.' She scribbles his name on her Intro to Education course notebook."

The couple obliges us by sitting on a bench 20 yards away. Jake picks up the love story where I left off. "But Brett—that's his name—had three dates last week, and this one, Sherry, isn't his favorite."

"And," I interrupt, "Sherry knows this deep down, that even while she's trying to impress him with stories about her high school homecoming dress, she'll never be good enough for Brett. So she goes back to talking about *him*—Brett's favorite subject. She realizes she's talking too much, but she can't stop herself."

"And all Brett can think of is the pot he left in the room, and that he'll kill his roommate if he touches it. Look at that!" Jake whispers. "He's giving you the once-over, Matt."

"He is not," I claim. But it's pretty clear he is. His gaze travels slowly up and down my body. "Let's move right along," I suggest.

Jake puts his finger over his lips, then points to the couple sitting in the grass a few feet from us.

I strain to hear what they're saying.

"Well, Megan said everyone will be there," the girl whines.

"Okay," the guy answers. "I said I'd go."

"I need to shop for something to wear to homecoming."

They don't talk for a minute. Then the guy says, "I gotta get my car checked. My brother's car is four years newer than mine, and he's four years younger than me."

"And shoes," she continues. "Shoes are even harder."

"I told my folks it's not fair. That kid gets whatever he wants."

"I haven't found a hair place here either."

Jake whispers, "It's like they're on different channels. Makes me dizzy."

We observe other couples. Jake claims he spots a Mafia hit man in love with his "target." I claim to identify the Princess of Monrovia in disguise, eloping with her bodyguard. We eavesdrop on conversations, listening to people whose dates aren't listening to them.

"It's like at that 21 Club, Jake," I complain. "I could have said anything. The guys weren't listening."

"I know. I like Stella—don't get me wrong. But I think I hear about half of what she says, and it doesn't make a bit of difference."

This surprises me because Stella and Jake are both great conversationalists. "I don't get it."

He explains. "Stella is so caught up in the homecoming elections that she doesn't want to talk about anything else."

I tell him a story I read about Franklin D. Roosevelt. "FDR hated White House receptions because he thought people were so busy trying to get on his good side that they didn't listen to him. So at this one international reception, as he shook hands with all the dignitaries, he smiled and said, 'I'm fine. I stabbed my grandmother to death this morning. How are you?' Man after man answered, 'Glad to hear that, Mr. President. Thank you for inviting me.' Until he got to one minor African official, who responded, 'Well, I'm certain she had it coming, Mr. President.'"

Jake laughs so loud, people turn and people-watch us.

Suddenly we're both quiet. I'm watching a drama unfold in front of us, as a couple makes its way through the quad. A tall thin guy stammers, "H-h-he d-d—"

"He didn't?" the girl asks. She's small and graceful. They walk slowly because she stops and looks up at him while he tries to get out sentences through his stutter. Neither of them seems frustrated with the process, but they're intense. He tells her about his prof, who wouldn't wait for him to answer a question in class, even though he was the only one who knew the answer.

She shakes her head and squeezes his arm. "He doesn't know you, Nick. The test will be essay, right?"

"R-right."

"Man, will you show him then!" She hugs him.

He hugs her back, and they walk off, holding hands.

Without a word Jake fishes into the postcard sack and comes out with a picture of a little girl squinting in concentration, holding a shell to her ear. He turns the card over and writes,

LOVE RULE #5
Love is listening. Really listening.

LOVE RULE #5

Love is listening.
Really listening.

EMMA JACKSON
RR 1
Hamilton, Missouri
64644

And for the first time since we've done this for Emma, I feel like we've landed on something.

Jake walks me back to my dorm. When we get there, I turn to him. "Emma's the best listener in the world, Jake. And she can't even hear."

Wednesday morning I have a mystery e-mail, with a quote from E.B. White.

> Being with you is like walking on a very clear morning—definitely the sensation of belonging there.

"I can't take it anymore!" I exclaim.

"Can't take what?" Gillian yawns and gets out of bed.

"I see Eric in the English department, and he barely looks at me. Then he sends me these e-mails, and I feel like I'm falling in love with him. Last week I told him in an e-mail how much I love E.B. White. And he listened, Gillian! He listened."

"So what are you going to do about it, girl?" She sounds fired up, like I am.

"I'm going to make that boy fess up."

Gillian loans me her green tank top and a black leather skirt I've never seen her wear. Then she helps me tame my hair. I'm as nervous as if I'm going on my first date.

On my way to the English department I ask God to give me the words that will make Eric listen. And I thank God for listening too.

*

The Grad Assistant

I stack Dr. Frost's graded tests on Mrs. Colton's desk and thank her for offering to file them for me.

"You're in a good mood," she comments.

I grin. "I guess I am. I think I'm getting another assistantship next year."

"Good for you!" she replies.

It's better than she realizes. Now that I know I wouldn't have to start out marriage deep in student loans, I'm planning on asking my girlfriend, Christy, to marry me. I turn to leave when I see the freshman work-study student walk in. I nod and keep going.

"Eric!" she calls after me. "Come back. I want to talk to you."

"Me?" I have to pick up student evaluations for Dr. Brigmon before sitting in on Professor Wolynski's class. "I'm kind of in a rush. Could we—"

She grabs my arm and pulls me toward the corner couch. Mrs. Colton gets up and leaves for the coffee room. "Now!" Mattie commands.

I follow her, but it makes me uneasy. I've suspected Mattie has a "crush" on me. Christy says I'm flattering myself, but I think I'm right. It's flattering and all, but sexual harassment is a trap I can't afford to get near. I take the chair next to the couch, and Mattie scoots all the way over.

She leans forward and stares intently. "Eric, I know."

"Excuse me?"

"Don't play dumb any longer. I know it's you."

"Okay," I answer. "What's me?"

"The e-mails! The English quotes? Don't pretend you don't know what I'm talking about. Emily Brontë? E.B. White?"

"Yes . . ." This is making me more and more apprehensive. I wish Mrs. Colton would come back in.

"So you admit it!"

"Admit what?" I ask. "Knowing Brontë and White? 'Guilty.'" I put air quotes around "guilty," so she can't use it against me in a sexual harassment suit. "So now, can I go?" I start to get up.

Mattie shoves me back into the chair. What if she's one of those stalkers? "Stay!" she demands. "We're having this out here and now. We know each other well enough after all those messages. You can admit it, Eric. I want us to have a face-to-face relationship. I'm tired of your mystery e-mails."

"You think I've been sending you mystery e-mails?" I don't know which is crazier—the girl in front of me, or the thought of my sending anybody anonymous e-mails. "Why would I do that?"

"Because you have a crush on me. You want to get to know me, and you're afraid—"

"Listen, Mattie," I interrupt. "Whoever's sending you e-mails, it's not me."

"Look, Eric. Just say it. Admit that you have a crush on me and—"

"*I* have a crush on *you?*" This whole thing is ludicrous. "Mattie, I'm twice your age."

"Hardly," she spits back.

I try for a fatherly smile. "I'm flattered. I'm sure you'll find someone your own age. And if we ever discover that 'Fountain of Youth,' maybe I'll wade in it and come back to see if you're still available. How's that?"

Her face reddens, and I don't know if it's from embarrassment or anger. She shoots up from the couch, like a spring just sprung. "Fountain of Youth? I'll tell you what, Eric Jensen. You don't need a Fountain of 'Youth.' You need a Fountain of 'Smart'!" She puts air quotes around "Youth" and "Smart." Then she races out of the office, slamming the door after her.

*

Mattie

I run all the way across campus. I've never been so embarrassed in all my life. How can I face Eric Jensen ever again? I feel like we've broken up. But we were never together! How pathetic is that?

It's not Eric. All that time, I was so sure.

And then it hits me. If my mystery e-mailer isn't Eric Jensen, who is it?

Instead of going into work, I log on to the computer and see if Emma's online. When she's not, I send her an e-mail.

```
:: Em ::
You are best friends with a total stupidhead!
It's not Eric. He's not my mystery e-mailer.
And now he thinks I'm crazy, which isn't far
from the truth. (What IS the distance between a
stupidhead and a crazy?). So, who? Who? Who?
Can't be Jeremy Skittles. No way. Who does that
leave?
```

Another message pops up. It's from my mystery man. I half-expect it to be Eric, apologizing for being such a coward. Maybe he's more afraid than I thought. I click on the message.

```
:: Dear Mattie ::
I hope your day is off to a good start. Mine
is. I just spent half the night rereading your
e-mails . . . and mine.

"I think I should have loved you presently and
given in earnest words I flung in jest."——Edna
St. Vincent Millay
```

Edna St. Vincent Millay? I love Millay. Who is this person reading my mind? I have to put an end to the mystery in Mystery Man. I click *Reply*.

```
This is it, Mystery Man. My last e-mail. I
can't play this game any longer. I will not
read any more messages from you unless you tell
me who you are. It's over. Call me right now
and arrange a face-to-face meeting, or stop
writing me. I know you're there, online. Call
now. Now or never.
```

I hit *Send*, sit back in my chair, and hope I've done the right thing.

For minutes I watch the second hand jerk slowly around Gillian's desk clock. I know it's crazy, but I feel like I've lost two loves in the span of one hour—first Eric, then my Mystery Man. I've scared him off. He's not going to call.

Ring! Ring!

I stare at the phone. It keeps ringing. Once more and voice mail will kick in. I snatch the receiver. "Hello?"

"Hi, Mattie. This is Carson."

Disappointment, like hot lava, pours through my bones. I slump back in the desk chair. "Oh. Hi, Carson. Listen. Could you call back later?" Mystery Man could be dialing right now. What if he doesn't have the courage to call back?

Carson doesn't answer or hang up.

"Carson? I'm waiting for a call. Sorry. Bye." I start to hang up.

"Wait! Mattie, wait!" Carson cries.

I replace the receiver to my ear.

"Mattie, the call you're waiting for? I'm it."

"I still can't believe my Mystery Man is Carson Vandermere."

It's Monday night, and Jake and I are stretched out against our sand dune. The tide is coming in hard. I managed to put off my in-person date with Mystery Man Carson until next weekend. I needed time to adjust. Never—not even once—did I suspect that he was the one writing those e-mails. I've pumped Jake to see if he knew. He hasn't admitted it, but I think he did. He's been quiet since he picked me up.

"Carson and I are going to some frat party next Saturday, a dance."

"I know." Jake looks like he's a million miles away.

"Jake, is something wrong? Is it Stella?"

"Huh? No. We're still seeing each other. We'll be at that frat dance too."

"Cool. At least I'll know a couple of people. And I do like to dance."

He turns and grins. "You *do* like to dance."

"Carson Vandermere," I say for what might be the thousandth time. Gillian has warned me that if I do it again, she's switching rooms. "And all this time, I thought that deep down, the guy was shallow."

Abruptly Jake takes out the postcard sack. "Let's do it, Matt."

I wrack my brain for a Love Rule. "I've been thinking about Carson all week, so I haven't come prepared," I admit. "Maybe this would be a good time to steal something from I Corinthians 13. That whole definition works—love is patient, love is kind." Then I remember the part that blew me away when I reread the chapter. "Or listen to this, Jake. 'All that I know now is partial and incomplete, but then I will know everything completely, just as God knows me now.' Isn't that cool? How God knows us totally?"

I'm not sure where I'm going with this, so I think out loud. "I was such a stupidhead for thinking I'd fallen in love with somebody I didn't know at all, someone who didn't know *me* either. Don't you think, at the very least, you have to know someone before you love them?"

Jake doesn't answer, but he picks out a card. And without looking at the picture, he writes,

LOVE RULE #6
Anybody who falls in love with someone they don't know is a stupidhead.

I flip the card over to see the picture. It's the Flying Squirrel, symbol of Freedom University. Close enough.

For the rest of the week, I add an eating disorder to my sleeping disorder. I'm so nervous about going out with Carson that my stomach threatens to toss back anything I toss in. I try to think of Carson as Carson the e-mail friend I've come to know so well, not Carson the Greek God.

Eric and I successfully play keep-away in the English department. And I work Thursday to make up for not going in last Wednesday.

Saturday night it's a group project to get me gussied up. Naomi puts on my makeup. Laura and Gillian let me try on everything in their closets. We settle on a sleeveless white boatneck shirt. I opt for Gillian's black pleated skirt, so I can dance without ripping anything. It takes all four of us to fix my hair.

"So, Mattie," Naomi asks, stepping back to get a good look at her creation, me, "can you dance?"

"Can lovers leap?" I reply. "Can French kiss? lions share?"

"I get it. You can dance." Naomi makes me spin around for a last-minute inspection. "Good. Now, go get 'em."

I wait outside for Carson. It's a nice night, clear sky. Dates are beginning all around me. Then I see Carson strolling up the sidewalk. I think I'd forgotten how classically handsome Carson Vandermere is—which makes it even more amazing that he took all that time to get to know me through our e-mail messages. Watching him walk up, I feel something stir inside me.

"Hi, Mattie." Carson slowly leans down and kisses me, a short, soft kiss. "There. That's out of the way."

I grin. But it's like the kiss doesn't leave my lips.

"Got your dancing shoes?" He steps back and gazes at my feet. In answer, I do a little soft-shoe shuffle. "Lead on."

He takes my hand and starts walking. "It's such a beautiful

night," Carson begins, "that I thought it would be nice to walk. Do you mind?"

I love walking. "That's great, Carson." I keep my hand in his, and it feels good, warm, but not sweaty. I hope mine feels as good. The full moon is rising, although the only star we can see is Polaris. I'm holding hands with a guy who knows me and cares about me. And I wonder if this feeling, the warmth, then chills coursing through my body, if this is love.

Mystery Man

So far, so good. Mattie totally fell for the "It's-a-nice-night-let's-walk" routine. Now, if I can remember all the things Jake told me about her, everything he told me to write in those e-mails, or wrote himself, I'll be in good shape.

Jake really let me down this week, though. When I started the mystery e-mails, he was so into it. He couldn't stop talking about Mattie, what she liked, what she didn't. He even looked up quotes from her favorite authors or poets or something. Truth is, the dude wrote most of the e-mails himself.

Then all of a sudden, he shut down and left me stranded. He kept ragging on me to tell Mattie the truth. I was trying to wait until homecoming to reveal myself and ask Mattie to go to homecoming with me. But I guess it was a good thing she forced my hand. I'm pretty sure Jake would have gone back on his promise and told her himself sooner or later. I'm glad the whole boring business is finally over.

"Sure it's not too far for you to walk, Mattie?" We breeze across the quad. But I know her answer. Jake told me she loves to walk. He didn't tell me everything though. I had another source of info on Matilda Mays.

"I could walk to the beach," Mattie assures me. "I love to walk."

I go back to thinking about my other source of Mattie info, Valerie Ramsey. Now there's someone else I wouldn't mind hooking up with. Anyway, turns out she went to school with Mattie. Jake's little Matt has a lot more potential than I thought. Back in Missouri, Mattie had quite a reputation. Runs in the family, Valerie said. My hopes are high for tonight.

"Do you think so?" Mattie smiles up at me. She's been talking, but I haven't been listening.

I take a stab. "Yeah."

"Good. Me too," she continues. "And I have to hand it to you for hanging in there this long and letting me know what's going on inside you. After our cafeteria date, it must have taken a lot of nerve to even see me again. I guess we just didn't know each other well enough, huh?" She stops and points to the sky. "Carson, look! See it? What did you write about that constellation?"

I know zero about stars and care even less. Any star talk must have come from Jake. I shrug.

"Cassiopeia," she explains. "Remember? You said you always thought of it as a W instead of an M?"

I nod, like I'm remembering, then change the subject, quick. "Mattie, did I ever tell you about my last game of high school football?" Relating that victory takes up the rest of the walk. Finally I hear the music blaring from the ATO house. They're off campus, which makes them safest for keg parties.

As we cross the lawn, I call hi to every girl I know, which is a lot. Mattie doesn't seem to know anybody.

Inside, I find a group of pledges and their dates. Mahoney's date is so hot that if Mattie weren't with me, I'd risk hitting on her. I make small talk with her and at least get the name of her sorority. "I forgot to introduce my date," I tell Mahoney, giving his date the Vandermere smile. "Mattie—"

When I turn back to Mattie, she's not there.

Jake

Stella's telling me about the shoes or sandals she bought for home-coming. I've gotten good at smiling and making listening noises, just like the couples Matt and I spied on.

But I'm watching Matt. When she walked into the frat house, every head turned. And she didn't even notice. Matt has no idea that she changes the atmosphere of rooms she goes into, as if she's bringing the oxygen we all forgot we needed.

I watch as she slips away from Carson and ends up helping Alice, the cook here. Matt sets out bowls of nuts and throws away trash. She and Alice are laughing about something. I've seen Matt form instant friendships with traffic cops, Wal-Mart checkout ladies, construction workers, bus drivers, gas-station attendants, janitors . . . the list goes on forever.

When Carson finally spots Matt talking to Alice, he rushes over and almost drags her onto the dance floor. Matt closes her eyes and loses herself in the beat. Emma says Matt's a born dancer. I think she may be right.

"She's really good, isn't she?" Stella comments.

"What? You mean Matt? Yeah. She and Emma had dance routines worked out." I don't tell her that, usually, I was part of those routines.

"Let's dance, Jake," Stella suggests.

We move onto the dance floor, and I go through the motions. The next song is a slow dance. I hold Stella close. Her hair is soft, and she smells like flowers and cinnamon. Over Stella's shoulder, I see Carson and Matt. Carson's hand moves down Matt's back, stroking her like she's a cat. He pulls her in tighter. Matt steps back and smiles at him. Then they're dancing slow again. And I get a pain in the pit of my stomach.

When she sees me, Matt's eyes narrow, and her lips form a slight grin. Then she lifts her arms above her head, swaying with the music. And her fingers spell out, *Can I trade this date for what's behind Door Number 2?*

I crack up laughing.

"Jake, what's so funny?" Stella asks.

"I think Matt's in trouble. Do you mind if I get her away from Carson for one dance?"

"Good idea." Stella and I stop dancing. She's no fan of Carson Vandermere herself. "I'll run to the washroom while you save her."

I watch Stella walk off. Then I make my way over to Carson and Matt when the song ends. "Mind if I cut in?"

Carson scowls. We've been at each other all week. Then he manages a fake smile. "As long as it's not a slow dance, dude."

Matt grins at me. I have a feeling we're both thinking the same thing. I dash over to the band, three guys who look like they're refugees from high school. The leader comes over.

"Do you guys know 'Boogie-woogie Bugle Boy from Company B'?" I ask.

I get a blank stare for an answer.

I run through half a dozen songs they don't know until we hit on "Rock Around the Clock."

Matt's there when I turn around. I grab her, lift her off the ground, and swing into the jitterbug. Around us, couples try to rock and roll. But they fade away. Matt's smile is never bigger than when we're swing dancing. I spin her over my shoulders, between my legs, across my back. We slip into a Charleston step, side-by-side. I throw myself into it, until there's nobody here but Matt and me, the music, this dance, and maybe a little of Emma's God.

The song comes to an end, and we move to our big finish, keeping in perfect step with each other, as Matt spins into my arms, and I rock her back until her hair brushes the ground. It's the most fun I've had since I've been at school.

Applause breaks out around us with hoots and cheers. I hadn't even noticed that the floor cleared, just like in the old dance movies.

A couple of ATOs pat me on the back. One of them shakes his head. "Where did you learn to dance like that, man?"

"His little sister taught us," Matt shoots back.

Carson shoves his way in and puts his arm around Matt. "Thanks very much, dude. I'll take my date back now."

I find Stella, but I keep an eye on Matt. I don't trust Carson, and I don't like Matt being alone with him. If he doesn't tell her the truth about the e-mails, I will. I could kick myself for being a part of that mess. It felt like a prank when we started it. And I thought Matt deserved the extra attention, that it might make her feel good about herself to know she had a Mystery Man who had a crush on her. But it went too far.

And then, when I started answering the messages myself, instead of coaching Carson, and when Matt wrote back . . . I guess I was hooked. She wasn't just my little sister's friend anymore. I waited for those e-mails. I wanted to keep answering them.

Stella taps my arm. "Jake, I want you to meet Melissa. She's up for homecoming too."

I tell Melissa I'm glad to meet her. Then I let them talk about dresses and shoes and whether or not they can carry a purse, while I watch Matt out of the corner of my eye. She sneaks back to the serving table and takes a big bowl of punch out of Alice's arms. Then she picks up around the table.

Finally Carson pulls her away, and they leave. The air changes, as if Mattie Mays has taken the fresh air with her.

✳

Not-Such-a-Mystery Man

"Let's get out of here, Mattie." I'm tired of sharing her. I've never waited this long to get a girl into bed with me.

"We've hardly danced at all, Carson," she complains. She sniffs the air. "How many beers have you had?"

"One, dude," I lie. "What did you expect me to do while you and Twinkle-Toes were showing off?"

"Sorry. I didn't think you minded."

I force another smile. "No. I liked it. Everybody thought that was really cool." Everybody except me. I don't know why Jake thought he had to show off with *my* date. It's not like *his* date is hard to look at. He's really changed lately. I'm already asking around for a new roommate.

I lead Mattie to the ATO parking lot, where I left my car this afternoon. There's no way I'm walking again. "Hop in."

"Is this your car?" She sounds impressed.

"This year's model. It's a Porsche."

"No kidding. Would you pop the hood?"

"What?"

She grins, takes the keys out of my hands, opens the door, and pops the hood herself. Then she peers under it. "That's what I thought. You've got the turbo—450 horsepower, with the V-8 engine." She shuts the hood and brushes her hands together. "Torque has to be at least 450 pounds at 2250 rpm. Six-speed transmission, right?"

I nod. The six-speed is about the only thing I've understood.

"I know they showed this SUV back in 2002, at the Paris Motor Show. But I've never seen one for real. Arctic silver is great too. Can I drive? You did have that beer, right?"

I've had several beers, so I let her drive. She steers us through back streets to get to the highway.

"Carson, do you have any granola bars in here?" she asks, as we near the underpass.

"Are you hungry?" I guess I could take her out to eat, but it's not why I'm here.

"No. That's okay. Never mind." She slows as we drive past some bums near the underpass. I check to make sure the doors are locked, and I wish she'd drive faster.

I've talked her out of going right back to her dorm. Instead I direct her to Swing Alley. When my dad went here, they called it "Lovers' Lookout."

"Pull up under that tree," I tell her. "It's got the best view." Ahead of us, down in the valley, the lights of the city shine.

She stops the car where I tell her to. "It's beautiful."

"So are you." I try to scoot closer, but the stick shift is in the way. I reach over it and put my arms around her. "I've been waiting a long time for this, Mattie." I start to kiss her.

"Carson, what's your favorite E.B. White essay?"

"My what?"

"I mean, we all love *Charlotte's Web*. But have you read 'Once More to the Lake'?"

I take a deep breath. If I say no, she might suspect I wasn't the one behind the e-mails. If I answer yes, she could trip me up, ask me what I thought about something in it. "I liked that Web one best."

"Or Brontë?" She won't let it go.

I can sense that I'm losing her. So I act really interested as she goes on and on about a book. She's so hot, even rattling on like an English teacher. Make no mistake about it. This girl drives me crazy. But letting her ramble is working. She relaxes. When I put my arm around her, she doesn't pull away. She even rests her head on my shoulder.

I move to the next level and trail my fingers down her arm until—

She scoots away and glares at me. "Carson, don't you remember what we said about getting to know each other first, before the physical gets in the way?"

"But I *do* know you, dude!" I insist. "And you know me."

She opens the door and gets out. I fumble with the latch, then follow her. She slips onto the front of the Porsche. So I do too. We lean against the windshield, and it's not comfortable.

Finally I can't wait any longer. I make my move. I roll over onto her and kiss her.

"What are you doing?" She shoves me so hard that I slide off the hood and fall to the ground.

"That hurt!" I cry. "What's with you, dude? I don't get it."

"You don't get it? You really *are* dumber than you look." She slides off the car and gets into the driver's seat. "I'm leaving, Carson. Now."

"Wait!"

The engine starts. She revs the motor.

I scramble off the ground and jump into the passenger seat half a second before she backs the car up.

"You're so different, Carson."

I can't believe this is happening, not after all the time I spent setting this up. I'm not giving up now. "Mattie, I'm sorry. See? This is exactly why I didn't want to tell you who was sending the e-mails, not yet. I'm having trouble controlling myself. I—I care too much. I don't know how to act around you." I can't tell if I'm getting through to her. "You have to think of me as the guy who wrote all those e-mails. Remember, Mattie? Remember how close we were getting?"

She keeps driving, but she won't talk. Then she stares at me, as if trying to figure out who I am.

Neither of us speaks again until she pulls up in front of her dorm and shuts off the engine. Then she studies me. "Carson Vandermere, it's like you're two different people."

I shoot for a sheepish grin that works on most girls. "That's me—Schizophrenic Carson."

She gets out of the car, then leans in the window. "Well, at least you'll have each other."

I vault over the stick shift and hustle up the walk after her. "Wait! Mattie! When do you want to go out again?"

She stops, then turns toward me and calmly answers, "Never. How about never, dude? Is never good for you?"

"Have a heart, Mattie," I beg, putting my hands on her shoulders. "Give me another chance. I know I screwed up here. I'm going to hate myself in the morning." I can feel the Carson charm thawing her. The magic is working.

Mattie carefully lifts my hands off her shoulders and sweetly replies, "Carson, don't hate yourself in the morning. Sleep in."

Then she disappears into her dorm.

Women.

Mattie

Emma, I just had that date with Mystery Man,
aka Greek God, aka Carson Vandermere III. What
a letdown! We should have stayed in cyberspace.
Maybe oxygen doesn't agree with him. Maybe
it turns him into an octopus. He was all over
me. And I didn't want him to be. For a while,
Em, when he showed up and wanted to walk, when
we held hands, I thought what I was feeling
might be love. But it couldn't have been,
could it? When I thought Eric was my Mystery
Man, I had that feeling, that stirring,
whenever I was around him. What's up with
feelings anyway?

I'm going to reread everything you've sent me
about love. Will you e-mail me the Love Rules
Jake and I sent you too? Because I'm feeling

```
like I know even less about love than I did
before I came here.

Love (whatever that is), Mattie
```

Later that night, an e-mail pops up from Carson. At least he's signing his own e-mails now. It takes me a while to get up the nerve to read it.

```
Please forgive me, Mattie. Give me another
chance? I won't drink. I'll be your e-mail
Mystery Man. I know we can work this out. When
I watched you walk into the dorm, I felt like
I'd lost you. The way to love anything is to
realize that it might be lost.
———G.K. Chesterton. I can't lose you. It would
be like losing myself.

So, can you forgive me? Even Shakespeare knew
this love stuff wouldn't be easy: The course
of true love never did run smooth.
```

When I shut down the computer, I feel as if I've been tag teamed. Chesterton and Shakespeare? My feelings for this "Mystery Man" come flooding back, filling some hole inside me. I want to believe him. I want to be loved.

I'll give him one more chance.

Sunday night, Gillian and Michael are IMing, and I horn in with questions for them.

"Okay, you two," I begin. "How did you guys know you were in love?"

Gillian types in my question, then reads Michael's responses, and hers, aloud. "It's more than a feeling, although there's that too," Gillian explains, typing her own words onto the screen. "But you don't always *feel* like you love somebody, not when they hurt you or do something dumb."

Michael types:

```
Ouch!  Kidding Gillian's right. I always love
her. Nothing she could do would change that, no
matter how I felt. Feelings come and go. But
I've chosen to love this woman.
```

We stay at it for another hour, and I think Michael and Gillian must be the luckiest two people on earth. Or maybe it's not luck.

*

Jake

Monday, I'm ready for postcard night an hour early. All week long I looked forward to picking up Matt and heading for our dune. Maybe she'll tell me about her date with Carson. Carson and I aren't speaking.

Stella and I see each other every day, even though she's wrapped up in homecoming, with the elections a week away. But I don't look forward to getting together with her. It's hard to explain because I'm not sure I understand it. Maybe Matt's right about the "Penultimate Plague." I built Stella up so much that nobody could measure up.

But I think something else is going on. I'm still attracted to Stella—that hasn't worn off. It's just that I don't like myself that much when I'm with her. I'm not real with Stella, not like I am with Matt.

Matt's waiting for me outside her dorm. She's wearing cutoff jean shorts and a white T-shirt, but she looks like she should star in a soap commercial. I take a minute and watch her before she sees me. Then I pull over and let her hop in.

"Hey, Jake! Time to put our seat belts on."

We do. Then I head for the beach, taking a small detour to

run by Albert. This time we both get out. I've got crackers and cheese to go with the granola bars. And bottled water. Last time I drove down here, Albert confided to me that he hates Gatorade but didn't want to hurt Matt's feelings.

"Thank you, Jake." Albert takes the bag from me. "You brought those crackers again."

"Again?" Matt asks.

"Ellen's real partial to those peanut butter ones you brought time before last." Albert smiles over at the woman, who always keeps her distance.

"I'll remember," I promise.

Matt looks confused. "When were you down here without me?"

"Your friend stops by now and again," Albert explains.

I'm not even sure why I did it the first time—probably the little Mattie voice in my head. But since then I've been stopping because I wanted to. Albert's a great guy.

Our dune is right where we left it. I spread out the blanket, and we dive onto it before the breeze snatches it away. I have to sit on the bag of postcards. We lie back and stare at the stars, and I feel more like myself than I have since last Monday.

"So how are you and Stella?" Matt shoves her hair behind her ears.

"Okay, Matt. I don't know. I haven't talked to her in several days."

She elbows me. "Don't tell me you're tired of Stella. You can't leave her hanging. She's nice."

"She *is* nice."

"And gorgeous," Matt adds.

"And gorgeous," I agree.

"So? Why haven't you called her in days?"

"I've called. But I didn't talk. Didn't want to interrupt."

"Jake! Stella's not like that."

I feel bad for talking about Stella. She's not the problem. I am. "I know. She's so caught up in this homecoming thing. She doesn't think she stands a chance of beating the other 11 candidates."

"She will," Matt assures me. "But what's up with having 12 candidates? I mean, why do we get 12 choices for homecoming queen, and only two for president of the United States?"

I laugh, and it's the most relaxed I've felt all week. We don't talk for a while. With Matt, I never worry about silence, not the way I do with Stella. A flock of starlings takes off from the shore. "Matt, look!" We watch the birds, maybe 30 of them, move together as if they're held inside a balloon, caught in the wind.

After a while, she asks, "What do you really think of Carson, Jake?"

I want to tell her everything—about Carson and the e-mails. But I promised Carson I wouldn't. To be honest, that's not what's keeping me from spilling everything to Matt, though. I don't think she'll understand why I did it. And she'll be fiery. I don't want her mad at me.

Matt snaps her fingers. "Beach to wherever you are. Never mind. We better do Emma's card before you fall asleep on me."

We dump the cards onto the blanket, sheltering them from the wind. The pile is a lot smaller than when we started back in August. I flip through them. "So, what's the Love Rule of the week?"

"Something about how love's not a gooey feeling?" Matt suggests.

"A gooey feeling?" I repeat.

"Like you had for Stella," Matt snaps.

"Like you had for Eric," I fire back. I can't bring myself to even tease Matt about feeling anything for Carson. I don't want her to. I'm not sure why. But I don't want her to.

"Gillian and Michael were trying to explain to me that you can't always trust your feelings, so love has to be more than that. What about something like, 'Love isn't a feeling'?"

I pass her the card with a big red heart on the front. We've been saving it for a rainy day, but she takes it and writes,

LOVE RULE #7
Love is not a feeling.

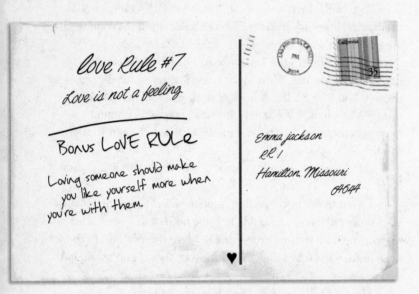

"That's pretty short." Matt holds up the card to moonlight. "Lots of space left for another rule."

I take it and write what I've been thinking about all week.

Bonus LOVE RULE
Loving someone should make you like yourself more when you're with them.

Matt takes the card and reads it. "Laura, my suite mate, should read this one. She really thought she loved Steve. But when she was with him, she felt rotten about herself. He made her feel inadequate. Or maybe she made herself feel that way." Matt stares over at me as if she's never seen me before. "Deep, Jake." But she's not making fun, not this time.

I grin. "I can do deep."

"You can indeed," she agrees.

We're on our way back to campus when I get up the guts to mention Carson. "So, Carson said you two have a date this weekend. Where are you going?"

"I don't know. He said I could choose." She gets her impish grin. "Maybe I'll teach him how to do carrot calls, and we can hunt rabbits." It's something she and Emma claimed to do when they were kids.

"That should be fun," I comment.

"Maybe. In cyberspace, Carson has a great sense of humor. In person, he's about as funny as cement."

I laugh, and it strikes me that nobody makes me laugh like Mattie Mays.

Mattie

I feel better after postcard night with Jake. Carson is Jake's roommate. That alone should be enough for me to give the guy another chance. Still, I'm not looking forward to our date. And it is definitely his last chance.

Tuesday morning, Emma e-mails me a list of all our Love Rules to date—

#1 The chances of finding love at this
university are slim to none. And Slim went
home.

#2 Love controls your mind and makes you think
constantly about the one you love.

#3 The one you don't want to call you will
always call, and the one you're dying to have
call you won't. So, maybe the secret to love is

```
not really liking the person you want to love
you.

Bonus: We want what we don't, or can't, have in
love. So, if you want someone to like you, stay
on the other side of the fence.

#4 The trouble with love in the real world is
that there's no background music.

#5 Love is listening, really listening.

#6 Anybody who falls in love with someone they
don't know is a stupidhead.

#7 Love is not a feeling.

Bonus: Loving someone should make you like
yourself more when you're with them.
```

I can remember every Monday night, and all the traumas that went into those rules.

That afternoon I buy a phone card in the bookstore and keep calling Mom until I get her.

Finally she answers. "Mattie? Are you all right?"

"I'm fine, Mom."

"Well, it's good to hear from you, honey."

I can tell (a) someone is in the room with her, and (b) she's been drinking. My first instinct is to hang up fast. I hate the way she is around men. But I think, *Love is not a feeling*, and I don't hang up. "How's your job, Mom?"

She lists off the same complaints I've heard a million times, mostly about her boss and Julie, who works with her and thinks she's better than everybody else.

When she stops talking, I say, "I just called to tell you I love you, Mom."

"You what?"

In the background a man shouts something to her, but I can't make it out.

"I love you," I repeat.

I hear her sniffing, and I'm pretty sure she's crying. I know she's drunk. And when she's drunk, she bawls over sappy commercials and bruised lettuce. But I feel warm tears in my throat too.

We talk a little longer, and I make her laugh, telling her about my visit to logic class and my job in the department. I leave out all mention of Eric Jensen, though. I tell her about some of the Love Rules Jake and I have sent to Emma. Twice, she tells whatever guy she's with to shut up because she's talking to her daughter.

I'm thinking we haven't talked this long since I was three years old.

The phone card warning breaks in, threatening to cut us off in two minutes.

"I'll call you next week, Mom," I promise. "Take care, okay?"

"You too."

The first thing I want to do after I hang up, besides blow my nose, is call Jake and tell him about the call. I dial his room. But when Carson answers, I freeze and hang up.

Saturday night, I keep dropping things while I'm getting ready to go out. Gillian offers to loan me her new black capris, but I choose my own jeans, the newest pair, and a red shirt I bought right before I left Missouri.

Carson calls up from downstairs. I don't know why I'm so nervous about this date with him. I start to leave. Then I come back and hug Gillian good-bye, as if I'll never see her again.

*

Jake

I broke my date with Stella. She didn't mind. She has a million things to do before homecoming elections on Monday. I've been telling myself I didn't want to go out with Stella tonight because I can't take another night of homecoming talk.

But that's not it. I want to be here when Carson comes back from his date with Matt. I can't get it out of my head. I watched him comb his hair, dash on cologne, and stick his fat wallet in his back pocket. He was actually whistling. I think I hate him.

"Aren't you going to wish me luck, dude?" Carson checked himself in the mirror one more time.

"Take it easy with Matt, Carson," I warned. "She's not like girls you're used to. And you ought to come clean with her about those e-mails too."

"Give it a rest, Jackson," Carson pleaded. He tossed his keys up, then caught them. "Don't wait up."

When the door closed behind him, I wanted to run after him, drag him back, and chain him to his desk. Is that so wrong?

I try pacing our room, until I can't take it anymore. So I go down to the courts and shoot hoops for two hours straight. Sweat pours off me. A couple of the guys come by and ask if I want to go get a pizza. But I have to be here when Carson gets back, so I turn them down.

Back in the room, I turn on the TV, but I can't follow anything. When I catch myself staring at some man selling spoons with holes in them, I turn it off. Then I'm too wound, so I pace again, feeling like I could explode from the inside out. I know what Em would do, and I wish I could too. I wish I could pray and let God do his thing for me like he does for Emma.

It's weird. I've wanted that more and more lately. It feels like I'm on the edge of a cliff and need to jump over to faith. It's not that I don't believe in God and Jesus and the whole bit. You can't live with Emma and think she's living a lie. I'm just afraid it wouldn't work for me—or I wouldn't work for it. I'd jump, make it, then lose all interest, like I do with everything.

Where are they? I check my watch and can't believe it's only 10 o'clock.

The door slams open, and Carson stumbles in. His hair is messed up, and the front of his shirt is stained. He's wasted.

"Carson, where have you been? Where's Matt? Is she okay?" I brush past him and check the hall to be sure she's not out there. "What happened?" I shut the door. "Where did you take her?"

Carson laughs. "Where? To Kiddie Land, of course. We played skeeball. Isn't that special?"

I can't help grinning. Carson hates little kids.

"She pretended she worked there." He slurs his words. "She walked around showing little brats how to win extra tickets. Special, special, special."

"Did you tell her about the e-mails?" I press. "You can't keep lying to her. I told you. Matt's not like other girls."

"Oh no. Not your little Matt." He sneers, and in that instant, I can't believe I ever thought this guy was my friend. "Maybe you don't know little Mattie as well as you think you do."

"You're drunk, Carson."

He mimes shooting a free throw. "Carson shoots. He scores!"

I get a sick feeling in my stomach. He's lying. Matt would never sleep with him. "Shut up, Carson. I know Matt. She wouldn't do it."

He grins. "Grow up, Jake. Your little Missouri girls sure have. That other one, Valerie Whatever, she's had more football players than the NFL. Did you know that?"

"You don't know what you're talking about." But I've heard the rumors about Valerie.

Carson takes off his shoes, nearly toppling over in the process. "So I don't know what I'm talking about? Well, maybe not when it comes to Valerie Whatever. Secondhand information on *that* Missouri girl." He smirks up at me. "But I've got firsthand info on your little Mattie. She's not bad either. Makes up in passion what she lacks in experience."

I shove him. "Shut up, Carson!"

He trips and falls back onto his bed, laughing. "She was ripe for the picking, Jake. The way you softened her up with that e-mail crap."

"I mean it, Carson! Shut up!" I don't want to hear this.

But he won't shut up. He keeps talking about Matt, about him, about them.

I can't shut him out. I can't keep his words from sinking into me. They cut into my chest, my heart, until I think I'm going to be sick and never feel right again.

Mattie

Sunday, I think about going to church. I know I need to find one. Gillian's gone home again, so I'm alone in my room. I want to block out all memory of Saturday night. Why did I think I had to give Carson Vandermere another chance?

I pull out my Bible and climb back into bed. I start with the "love chapter." When I get to the definition of love, I can't stop the images of last night with Carson from flashing through my brain.

"*Love is patient.*" Carson couldn't wait to get out of Kiddie Land and drive to his lookout—makeout—point above the city.

"*Love is kind.*" When I told him I didn't even want him to kiss me, he got nasty and pulled out his flask and started drinking. He called me cold and country and immature.

"*Love is not jealous or boastful or proud or rude.*" He was all of the above. I don't get it. He's so jealous of Jake and me. He said he never stood a chance, which is crazy.

I keep reading, fighting off the images of Carson growing more and more drunk, lashing out at me, telling me I wasn't worth the wait, that he has girls lined up, dying to go out with him.

I close the Bible. I want to talk to Jake. I want to tell him everything.

I start to dial Jake's room, but the fear of having Carson answer makes me hang up. So instead I turn on my computer and e-mail Emma.

```
:: Em ::
Carson Vandermere is no longer a mystery. I
never should have gone out with him again. The
date started out okay. I talked him into going
to this skeeball place. I had so much fun
teaching these little kids to score big. I kept
losing Carson, but I thought he was having a
good time too.
```

```
Then he said he wanted to leave. But instead of
taking me back to the dorm, like I asked him
to, he drove to that place overlooking the
city. It got pretty ugly, Em. Guess he's not
used to rejection. He drove 90 mph to drop me
off at the dorm, so he could go get drunk
somewhere "and find a babe who appreciates
him." So raise your thumb and index finger to
your forehead in a "Loser" salute and farewell
to Carson Vandermere III.
```

```
Better not say anything to Jake until I get a
chance to talk to him. I'm afraid he'll want
to beat Carson up—not that I think that's a
bad idea. But I don't want to get Jake in
trouble.
```

Monday night I stand outside to wait for Jake as usual. When it's a quarter after midnight and he still hasn't shown, I realize that this is the first time he's been late in weeks. A drop of rain, big as a bug, falls on my head. Then the sky opens, and rain pours down. Instead of running for cover, I stay where I am. I stand outside and let the rain beat on me until after 1 A.M.

I can't believe Jake would forget our postcard night. I thought it meant something to him.

Gillian is asleep when I finally get back to the room. I should get out of my wet clothes and warm up under my covers. But I don't want to go to bed and lie awake. I want to talk to Jake. I need to tell him about Carson. I guess I've depended on these Monday nights to keep my head together. I've looked forward all week to postcard nights. And now Jake hasn't even bothered to show up? How could he do that?

It's late, but it's stopped raining. I make up my mind. I slip back out of the room and run down the steps and across the quad to Jake's dorm, easing in with a group of guys who leave the door open. Nobody is on the stairs as I climb the eight flights to Jake's room. I knock until the door opens.

Carson sticks his head out, sees it's me, then scowls. "What are *you* doing here?"

"I want to talk to Jake."

"Jake's not here." Carson starts to shut the door.

I put my hand on the door to stop him. "Wait! Where is he?"

Carson sneers. "Where do you think he is? He's with Stella."

The door slams in my face. Tears trickle down my cheeks, so I must be crying. It's hard to breathe.

Jake is with Stella.

I race out of Jake's dorm, without even thinking about where I'm going. Behind the dorm, the basketball courts are empty. I see a ball in the grass, and I cross the yard and pick it up. Turning the wet basketball in my hands, I step onto the closest court and dribble. I shouldn't feel this way, and I can't explain it. Am I this upset because Jake forgot about our postcard?

Or because he's with Stella?

I dribble to my spot behind the free-throw arch, shoot, and score. Again and again—dribble, shoot, score—over and over, trying to keep thoughts out of my head. I try to convince myself that I'm mad at Jake for Emma's sake, because she counts on getting her postcard every week, because we promised her that much.

But it's more. It's Jake. I feel as if I've lost something huge in losing him.

I'm not sure I can handle feeling like this. And I wish other people were around. I'd impersonate one of them. I could pretend to be a groundskeeper or a cheerleader or a security officer—anyone except Mattie Mays.

I shoot baskets so long that my arms grow too heavy to lift the ball, and I collapse to the ground, still hugging the basketball. I look up into a half-moon, incomplete, alone, without a single star around it. *I don't want to be alone, God.*

I glance around. Nobody's in sight. It's just me. Except I remember the verse Gillian showed me when we were talking about love. It said something about being poor and needy, but knowing that God's thinking about me right now. *God*, I pray, *I really am poor and needy. I hate being needy. Are you thinking about me?*

It scares me to want God to be thinking about me, to need God this much. Mattie Mays, queen of other people's phobias, is afraid herself.

I'm scared, I admit to God, to myself. And it's almost like I hear the answer in another of Em's verses, one that she used to tell me over and over when we were still back in Hamilton together—*Perfect love expels all fear.* And I'm thinking that if God's love isn't perfect, then nothing is.

I hug the basketball to my chest and don't know whether to laugh or cry, because I think I'm starting to get it. God loves me—thinks about me, listens to me, makes me feel better about me, is patient, kind, everything we've discovered about love. That's how God is with me. And the cliché that's driven me crazy, the way everybody wants someone to "be there" for them—it's not a cliché with God. God's really here.

Exhausted, I curl up on the basketball court, on my spot, and I'm thankful for God's love. I still want a guy to love me. But this is good. And here, under a half-moon that glows with a silver rim and the outline of the whole, the promise of the whole I can't see, I fall asleep and have the best night's sleep I've had in California.

36

Tuesday morning I get to history class early so I can talk to Jake. There's so much I want to tell him. But he doesn't show. I keep an eye out for him on campus, but I don't go by his dorm. I don't need to see Carson again.

Tuesday night, while I'm filling Gillian in on what's happening—or rather, what's not happening—between Jake and me, Naomi strolls in. She's eating an orange, and the scent perfumes our room.

"Jake?" She comes in at the end of the conversation. "Are you talking about the breakup?"

"What breakup?" I ask.

"Jake and the homecoming queen." She laughs. "Sounds like a TV sitcom, doesn't it? Or a made-for-TV movie? 'Jake and the Homecoming Queen.'"

"Naomi," Gillian begs, "back up and start over."

"Stella, down the hall." Naomi's long nails pick out a seed from an orange section. "She won that homecoming thing. Then she and Jake broke up. That's what I heard."

"How could she do that?" I think about what Jake must be feeling right now. He was pretty crazy about her. "She won, so she dumps him?"

"Like a truck," Naomi answers.

"Are you sure?" Gillian asks. "I didn't think Stella was like that."

"You don't think anybody's like that," Naomi observes.

I turn to Gillian. "Maybe that's why he didn't come to class. He's too upset about Stella. What's wrong with her anyway? Jake's not good enough for her now?"

I storm to the door. "She can't do this to him. It's not right."

"Mattie?" Gillian calls after me.

But I don't stop. I practically run to Stella's and pound on the door until she answers.

"Mattie?" Stella frowns at me from the other side of the door.

"I need to talk to you." I walk past her, into her room.

"Sure. Come on in." She closes the door.

"I can't believe you won homecoming—"

"I couldn't believe it either," she interrupts. "They called, and—"

"What about Jake?" I cry.

She sighs and studies her fingers. Then she sits in her desk chair. "What *about* Jake?"

I stare at her. She's so pretty. But she's not too pretty for Jake. "I thought you liked Jake. He's going to be really messed up over this. He's thinking about dropping out of basketball. Midterms are coming up. And now this? How can you do this to him?"

She smiles at me. "How can I do this to him?"

"Right!" She's not this dumb. "How could you break up with him when—"

"Mattie." Her voice is calm, as if she's quieting a child. "*I* didn't break up with Jake."

"You didn't?"

She shakes her head. "Jake broke up with me."

"But—" I don't know what to say. Stella seems to be studying me. "Why? Why would he break up with you? I mean, he was so crazy about you, Stella. Are you sure?"

She grins. "I'm sure. Mattie, think about it. I'll bet you can figure it out. You're the genius. Skipped a grade. Valedictorian, full scholarship, aced your SATs."

"How did you know that? I haven't told anybody about that."

"Jake."

"Jake? He told you those things? About me?"

She sighs again. "He told me many things about you, Mattie. He talks about you all the time. Trust me. I ought to know." She walks to her door and opens it. "Mattie, I'm not the one you should be talking to about this."

I feel like a zombie as I walk to the door. It's too much information for me to process. I think I tell Stella thanks, but I'm not sure.

Back in my room, Gillian is waiting for me. "Hey, girl. This was downstairs for you." She hands me a box, big enough to hold a beach ball. It's as light as a beach ball. The label reads, *To Mattie Mays & Jake Jackson (only to be opened in the presence of both)*.

"Mattie, are you okay?" Gillian puts her hand on my arm. "It can't be anything bad, right? It's from Emma, your friend."

"What? No. No, I'm sure there's nothing wrong." I read the address again. "It's for Jake and me. We both have to open it."

Then I know what I have to do. I have to find Jake and talk to him. I want to tell him everything.

"I have to go," I say. "I have to go to Jake."

✻

Jake

I hate the way I feel. For two days I've ditched classes and stayed under the covers. Carson's hanging out with the ATOs all week. We've crossed paths a couple times, but we don't speak.

Monday night I couldn't face Matt. I don't believe Carson. I really don't. But if I looked at Matt, if I could tell she really had been with Carson, I don't think I could handle that. And it would be my fault for going along with the mystery e-mails for so long.

Someone knocks at the door. I ignore it. Someone knocks again, harder and louder.

I fling back my blanket and go open the door.

Matt's standing there, a big brown box in her arms.

I stare at her, and it feels like a fist is lodged in my chest. Neither of us speaks. I want to pick her up and tuck her under my arm like a football. I clear my throat. "Carson's not here."

"Good." She wrinkles her nose.

"Good?" I repeat.

"I don't ever want to see your roommate again."

I'm not sure what to say. Or feel. "That's not the way I heard it, Matt," I finally manage.

Her face reddens, and for that brief second, I'm scared. I'm afraid she's embarrassed . . . ashamed of what she and Carson have done. I want to turn back time.

"And exactly what have you heard, Jake?" There's an edge to her voice now. And the red in her face—it isn't from shame. I've seen Matt angry often enough. I should have recognized it. She's mad—not embarrassed, not ashamed. Mad, crazy angry.

"You and Carson weren't . . .?" I stammer. "I mean, you didn't . . ." Relief floods over me.

Matt stares at me as if I've grown another head. "Jake Jackson, what's wrong with you? How could you even think that? I can't believe you! You—you—"

"Stupidhead?" I offer.

"Exactly." She drops the box and takes off down the hall.

I run after her, but the box is in the doorway. I trip and fall on my face. "Matt!" I cry.

She turns back. "Jake?"

I know I better get her sympathy while I can. She's not going to let this one go. So I stay down, face to the stinking hall floor.

Matt kneels beside me. I feel her hands on my head. She turns my face toward her. "Jake, are you hurt?"

I open my eyes. "Only if you won't forgive me, Matt."

She lets my head go, and it smacks the floor. "You scared me, Jake! And I'm still mad at you. How could you believe Carson? Don't you know me by now? You really are a stupidhead."

"More than you know, Matt." I can't stand holding back any longer. I want her to know—even though she's not going to like it—that I was the one behind those e-mails. Not Carson.

"You couldn't possibly be more of a stupidhead than I think you are," she snaps.

"Matt," I begin, struggling to sit up, "Carson didn't write those e-mails. I did."

"You what?" she shouts.

"Listen to me, Matt."

She starts to get up. "I'm done listening to you, Jake. I don't even know who you are anymore."

"Matt, please!" I take hold of her arm. "Please, just hear me out. Please? Then if you want to go, I won't stop you."

She jerks her arm away, but she stays, back stiff, still kneeling on the hall floor.

"Carson was so hung up on you," I begin. "He kept badgering me with questions."

"And you *had* to answer." Her voice is sarcastic.

"At first, I admit it was fun. I didn't even realize I knew so much about you. And the e-mails . . . they just kind of happened."

"Right."

"What I mean is that, in the beginning, he did write the e-mails. Only I told him what to write."

"Why would you do that?" Her voice is filled with pain and hurt.

For a minute I can't answer, and I'm afraid I'm going to lose it. "I'm sorry, Matt. I never meant for any of this to hurt you. I thought it would be fun for you to have a mystery admirer. I thought you deserved someone who was crazy enough about you to write and try to get to know you."

She doesn't say anything. She doesn't look away.

"And after a while, when Carson got tired of it, I took over."

"Why?"

"Because I didn't want to stop." I've gone over this in my head a million times, rehearsing what I'd say when I finally told Matt the truth. Only none of it's coming out right. "Matt, I meant what I wrote in those e-mails."

"Sure you did." Her face is tight, without expression, her hair wild and frizzy around her face. She's beautiful.

"I did. You're an amazing person, Matt. I don't think I ever realized how amazing until you opened up in those e-mails. You stopped just being my little sister's friend, and you became something else, someone I really wanted to get to know. I lived for those messages. And our postcard nights."

She blinks, and I pray that I'm getting through to her. "How did you know the writers I like?" she demands. "The poets? the quotes?"

"Hey, I listen when you talk," I answer. "I think it's a Love Rule."

"So is being honest."

That one hurts because she's right. "I'm sorry, Matt. I—"

A group of guys walks by, laughing and staring at us. "Take it inside, Jackson," one of them jokes. "Get a room."

Matt stands up. "Did Emma know?"

I shake my head. "I never told her. She's pretty smart, though. She may have guessed what was going on."

Matt turns and starts down the hall. There's so much more I want to tell her. I scramble to my feet, but the box is in the way and I have to untangle my legs from it. "Wait! Matt! I need a moon check!"

"That wasn't playing fair, Jake," Matt says when we're in my car on the way to the beach. It's the first thing she's said to me since we left my dorm. "A moon check?"

"I was desperate, Matt." I grin at her, but she doesn't return the grin. She's clutching the box on her lap as if she thinks I might steal it. "So what's in the box?"

She doesn't answer, so I punch on the inside car light and

check out the label. It's to Mattie and me from Emma. "What do you think it is?" I ask, trying to get her to talk to me. She doesn't respond. I take one more look before turning off the light. Emma's scrawled in big, black letters, *only to be opened in the presence of both*.

I love my sister. *Thank you, Em.*

✳

Mattie

I keep ahead of Jake as we walk to the dune, where we've sat nearly every Monday night since school started. The beach looks the same, but different, as if it's changed as much as I have in the last 24 hours. So many thoughts are swirling through my head. Jake sent the e-mails. Not Carson. I'm mad at him for not telling me. But somehow, when he did tell me, I didn't feel shock, or surprise. It was as if I'd suspected, without really suspecting.

None of it makes sense. I want to talk to Em, to see what she thinks of all of this—of Jake and me. The things I'm feeling for Jake, the way it hurt me to think of him with Stella . . . something's changed. Jake is not just Em's brother anymore. In my mind, I see Em grinning, the way she does when she's known things for a long time and has been waiting and waiting for us to catch up with her.

"Are you ever going to forgive me, Matt?" Jake asks for about the tenth time since we left his dorm.

Jumbling inside my head, with everything else, are the Love Rules we've sent Emma. If Jake hadn't stood me up on Monday, my next Love Rule was going to be, *Love means forgiving.* I'll forgive Jake. Maybe I have already. But I want us to get everything out in the open.

"I broke up with Stella," he says.

Finally I turn and look at him. Moonlight streaks the water and sends a glow off Jake's cheek. I'm not sure I ever realized how incredibly handsome he is. "I know you broke up with Stella, Jake."

"You do?"

I nod. "What I don't know is why."

Jake stares at me, his brow furrowed. "Because I'm figuring something out, Matt. Yeah—even stupidheads figure things out after a while."

I feel myself grin, but I fight it off. I'm not letting him off the hook. Not yet.

"Last week," Jake continues, "I had Emma e-mail me a list of the Love Rules we'd sent her. She added a couple of her own, by the way."

Emma Jackson. She did know. I'd had her do exactly the same thing, send me our Love Rules.

"I read the rules, Matt, and they didn't fit Stella. She's great. Don't get me wrong. But I don't love her. We barely listen to each other. I don't like myself that much when I'm with her. She's not the one I think about all day and night."

Jake moves closer, and I can hardly breathe. "*You're* the one I think about, Matt. I never thought of Valerie like that. Or Stella. Only you. The best minutes I've had at school have been the times we've been together. If you don't forgive me, if you don't want to see me again, I don't think I can stand it."

Something inside of me warms, melts. "I forgive you, Jake." I let myself smile at him and get lost in his big eyes. "I have to. This week's Love Rule is *Love means forgiving*."

"I like it." He smiles back at me, not looking away.

"Yep. *Love means forgiving, even when the other person is a stupidhead*."

"Another nice sentiment," Jake observes. "You could have a future in greeting-card writing, Matt."

He looks worn and spent, like he's squeezed out every bit of truth that was in him. He's been honest with me. I need to be honest with him.

"Matt," Jake says, before I can get a word out, "you're an amazing person. I want to be you when I grow up."

"No, you don't," I object. "Trust me. I don't think *I've* even wanted to be me. Growing up in my house, with my mom, it came in handy to transform into somebody else when I needed to." I look at him and know he's listening, really listening. So I don't stop. I tell Jake everything I've been thinking in the last 24 hours. I tell him about my night on the basketball court and how I figured out that the first place to find love is with God.

"See," I continue, "I've always been able to be, to imperson-ate, people—professors, security guards, waitresses, just about any-body, except myself. I'm not very comfortable in my own skin. But I'm starting to get it, that God loves me anyway. I can be myself with God. And with you." I turn to Jake, wanting him to under-stand. "I was afraid, I guess. I didn't want to need God—or anybody. But I do. And somehow, knowing that makes it not so scary. That's what I wanted to tell you, Jake."

He's staring at me so intently. "I've been thinking about God too, Matt. How can you not, with Emma as a sister?" He grins. Then it fades. "But what if I throw myself into God, and it ends up like everything else I do? A letdown. I'm cursed with the Penultimate Plague, remember?"

"It won't be that way, Jake. God's different. You can't put God up on a fake pedestal because he's already on a real one. He doesn't disappoint you."

Jake nods, and I think he gets it, that he's making that leap. I want to hold him and leap with him. Then he leans down and kisses me, soft and long.

We come apart, and I think we're both surprised. Jake grins and runs his fingers through his hair. "You suppose that one day we'll both look back on that kiss and laugh?"

"And then change the subject and talk about the weather?" I add. I scoot closer to him, and he puts his arm around me and kisses me again.

"Nah," he says, leaning back, keeping his arm around me so I'm nestled in the crook of his arm, a perfect fit.

We sit like that, watching the moon and listening to the waves slap the beach like wild applause.

"Hey, what about Em's box?" Jake reaches over me and pulls the box onto his lap.

I help him yank off the string, and we rip open the package. Inside the cardboard it's autumn. The box is filled with leaves. Even in the dark, I can see red and yellow maple leaves, mixed with oranges, and that burgundy color Em loves. I can smell burning leaf piles and evergreen and a hint of lavender. "Oh, Emma," I murmur, feeling, almost, like she's right here with us.

Without a word Jake and I stand up, each holding a box flap. Then we fling the leaves into the salty air and let them waft down around us, carried on a sea breeze, dancing to the ocean music. We stand together, under the moonlight, laughing in a leaf shower on the beach, sure of the promise that love rules.

About the Author

Dandi Daley Mackall has published over 350 books for children, teens, and adults, with sales of three-and-a-half million in 22 countries. In addition to *Love Rules*, she's also written *Sierra's Story* in the Degrees of Betrayal series for teens and *Kyra's Story* in the Gold Medallion nominee Degrees of Guilt series for teens (both Tyndale). Her young adult fiction best sellers include eight titles in the Winnie the Horse Gentler series (Tyndale), including *Wild Thing, Eager Star, Bold Beauty, Midnight Mystery, Unhappy Appy, Gift Horse, Friendly Foal*, and *Buckskin Bandit*. She was creative director of the teen fiction series *TodaysGirls.com* (TommyNelson) and author of *Portrait of Lies* and *Please Reply!* in that series. Her young adult novel *The Eve of Poland* (Harcourt) will be released in 2005. She's also written three nonfiction books for high school students on having success in the workplace: *Problem Solving, Teamwork*, and *Self-Development* (Ferguson).

Currently Dandi conducts writing assemblies and workshops across the U.S. She writes from rural Ohio, where she lives with her husband, Joe, and three children—Jen, Katy, and Dan—as well as two horses, a dog, a cat, and two newts. You can visit Dandi at dandibooks.com.

areUthirsty.com

well . . . are you?

fiction.

THE LAMB AMONG ✦ THE STARS SERIES

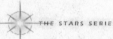

Other thirsty(?) fiction

thirsty(?) is a trademark of Tyndale House Publishers, Inc.

nonfiction.

Walk 0-8423-6069-7

Come Clean 0-8423-8358-1

Walking with Frodo 0-8423-8554-1

Walking with Bilbo 1-4143-0131-6

tap into life.

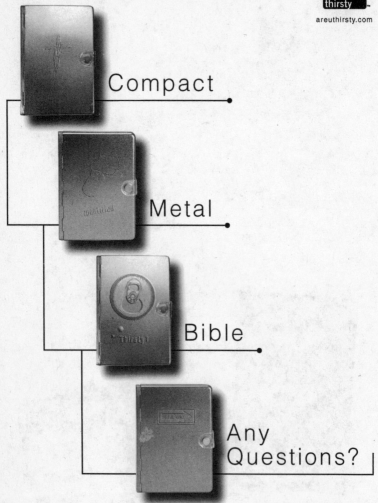

Compact

Metal

Bible

Any
Questions?

Available wherever Bibles are sold